Running Out of Night

SHARON LOVEJOY

Running out of Night

A YEARLING BOOK

Text and map copyright © 2014 by Sharon L. Lovejoy
Cover art copyright © 2014 by Meagan Bennett

All rights reserved. Published in the United States by Yearling, an imprint of Random House Children's Books, a division of Penguin Random House LLC, New York. Originally published in hardcover in the United States by Delacorte Press, an imprint of Random House Children's Books, New York, in 2014.

Yearling and the jumping horse design are registered trademarks of Penguin Random House LLC.

Grateful acknowledgment is made to Patrice Vecchione and Palanquin Press/Community Publishing for permission to reprint "Bless" from The Knot Untied. Reprinted by permission of Patrice Vecchione and Palanquin Press/Community Publishing (2013).

The spelling and treatment of common names of bird species follow Merriam-Webster's Collegiate Dictionary, 11th edition.

Visit us on the Web! randomhousekids.com

Educators and librarians, for a variety of teaching tools, visit us at RHTeachersLibrarians.com

The Library of Congress has cataloged the hardcover edition of this work as follows:
Lovejoy, Sharon.
Running out of night / Sharon Lovejoy. — First edition.
pages cm
Summary: "Journey of an abused twelve-year-old white girl and an escaped slave girl who run away together and form a bond of friendship while seeking freedom" — Provided by publisher.
ISBN 978-0-385-74409-6 (hc) — ISBN 978-0-375-99147-9 (glb) — ISBN 978-0-385-37846-8 (ebook) [1. Friendship—Fiction. 2. Runaways—Fiction. 3. Fugitive slaves—Fiction. 4. Race relations—Fiction. 5. African Americans—Fiction.] I. Title.
PZ7.L956045Ru 2014
[Fic]—dc23
2013026375

ISBN 978-0-385-37847-5 (pbk.)

Printed in the United States of America

10 9 8 7 6 5 4 3

First Yearling Edition 2016

To Sara May, Moses John, and Luke Edwin Arnold;
and to Ilyahna and Asher Prostovich—
you're the brightest stars in my sky.
Thank you for lighting my way.

Lark and Zenobia's Journey to Auntie's Cabin

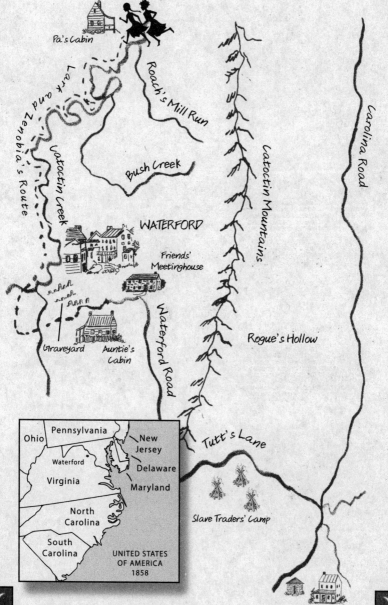

Pa's Cabin

Lark and Zenobia's Route

Roach's Mill Run

Bush Creek

Catoctin Creek

WATERFORD

Friends' Meetinghouse

Catoctin Mountains

Carolina Road

Graveyard

Auntie's Cabin

Waterford Road

Rogue's Hollow

Tutt's Lane

Slave Traders' Camp

Ohio | Pennsylvania | New Jersey
Waterford | | Delaware
Virginia | | Maryland
North Carolina
South Carolina | UNITED STATES OF AMERICA 1858

Emma and Little Will's Home

Could this be the beginning of something?
Will hatred have to back up
an inch or two, stumble, then slink
behind the corner, shamefaced?

—PATRICE VECCHIONE, "BLESS"

꒱

*Memories must be tended like a fire,
elstwise they'll die.*

Mama give her last breath just as I took my first.

Although Pa and my big brothers never said they blamed me for her death, I always felt it achin inside me, like the rotten tooth our blacksmith pliered out of my mouth. Why else would a pa and his boys let a little girl come into the world and live for twelve years without givin her a name?

My brothers and Pa always looked through me, as though I weren't but a thin sheet of mica between them and the world. Sometimes I had to step outside to see my shadow afore I knowed for sure that there were a real person inside me.

Even though I never knowed Mama, I pieced her together in my head the way I made my patchwork rag doll, Hannah. After my grandpa passed and his stories about my mama quieted, I grabbed on to the threads of Pa's and my brothers' mentions of her, which weren't often, and needled them into my own life.

*Stop a sneeze before it comes to the table
or death will visit soon.*

"Girl!" Pa shouted, and slammed his fist on the table. "More scrapple. I tole you plenty of times, I don't want nothin useless on my farm. You'd best start earnin your keep."

"My farm," he'd said, but as long as I were alive, it would always belong to my grandpa. Pa never worked the farm; he were born tired and raised lazy.

I scrambled acrost the dark kitchen and scraped the leavins out of the iron skillet and onto his plate. Pa never looked up or thanked me. He leant low over his food, turned his spoon sideways, and pushed big chunks of greasy scrapple into his mouth.

I hid my eyes behind a curtain of hair and looked for the best way out. Though I knowed every bit of this kitchen, from the ceilin beams hung with herbs to the wide pine floorboards, I needed a clear pathway, free of guns and legs. When Pa got into one of his moods, I had to get out of his way—and fast. I felt the hot flush move up my neck and flare into my cheeks the way it always does when I am mad. I didn't want Pa to feel my scairt or see my mad or I'd get kicked like one of the huntin hounds.

I might not have worked out in the fields, but I weren't lazy. I were the one who cooked our food, kept up the cabin, done the washin, mended, and tended our garden and animals. I squared my chin and bit down on my tongue to keep it from waggin me into trouble again.

My brothers and Pa left the table without a word; the door left open behind them. They walked out onto the porch, and Delia and Bathsheba, Grandpa's hounds, uncurled, shook, and loped after them. I heard a round of barkin and yippin, as though the hounds thought they was goin on a coon hunt.

I stood at the window and watched till they passed my tomater patch and turned the corner at the barn; then I pulled Mama's quilt off my bed and took it outside. I shook it good, spread it out along the porch rail to air, and run my hand over its fineness. My mama had worked the straightest, tiniest stitches into her quilts, but my needlework on my old pieced Hannah doll, it looked like the jaggedy scar that runs up the side of my leg.

I went back indoors and sank down onto the three-legged stool. The long cherrywood table, cut and milled on Grandpa's land and built by him, were strewn with food and grease. Grandpa, my mama's father, had been the onliest piece of softness in the family, a big, curly-headed Irishman who called me Girl like all the others, but when we was alone, my name were always Sweet Girl. And when we was alone and I cried over the things Pa and my brothers done to me, well, Grandpa always told me that bad beginnins are a sign of a good endin. I hoped I didn't have to wait too long for the good to come.

Grandpa teached me what I knowed about the stars—turned them from strangers to friends. He showed me how to plant by the moon and what wild herbs were for pickin and eatin, healin or hurtin. He learnt me how to shoot a gun till I were near as good as him. By my eighth birthday, I could hit a corncob stuck on top of the fence clear acrost the barnyard. He knowed all the animals and how to talk to them and care for them. He give that charm over to me to carry on. Two years ago, on the day he died, I felt like most of my world, leastwise the good parts of it, went into the grave with him.

I needed to pay Grandpa some respect. After I finished up the breakfast mess, I'd clean his table proper-like and work some of my beeswax into it to bring on a shine.

I picked up my sand bucket and lye, but afore I began scrubbin the floors, I set down and leant on my elbows. "Mama," I said aloud, "I made it safe through this mornin without gettin into trouble." My stomach grumbled. I slid some of the leftovers off of Pa's and my brothers' plates and sopped up the juices and grease with a heavy piece of yesterday's corn bread. "Thanks, Mama," I said. "You remembered my birthday and made me a cake." I closed my eyes, gnawed into the corn bread, and smiled. It tasted like angel food.

From outside, I heard somethin scuffle acrost the front porch. I jumped up and tucked the last of the dried-out bread into my pocket alongside some minty wintergreen leaves and the lucky buckeye Grandpa had always carried with him. Lord save me if Pa ever found me sittin down in the middle of the day. I blanked my face, smoothed my apron, and picked up a pile of dirty plates. The sound come again. I walked toward the door, then stopped mid-stride and listened. Catoctin Crick, so much a part of my life that I don't usually hear its noisesomeness, filled the cabin with its rain-fed roar.

The floorboards thrummed under my bare feet as someone walked along the porch, then stopped near the Catalpa tree. I stood, plates askew, cocked my head like a hooty owl, listened. Then I shivered. My head prickled like it did this mornin when my brother Samuel sneezed at the table—a sure sign of death comin soon.

*When you see a buzzard fly over your house,
you can be sure that company will soon arrive.*

The oak plank door shuddered, and then a dry *scritch, scritch, scritch* moved up and down, side to side, like twigs on a windowpane. I weren't expectin no one, but a big black buzzard flew over me this mornin when I were bringin in the firewood, so I knowed company were comin.

Not but two days ago three starvin Indians out huntin deer was killt by a settler who claimed they was stealin food from his land. We all knowed that it wouldn't be long afore some of our folks would be hurt, or killt, for what Blackburn had done to them Indians. Was they on my porch right now?

I set down the plates and crept toward the door. When I laid my ear against it, I heard a strange whimperin cry.

Someone or somethin were hurt out there, or lost, or sick, and I needed to gather up my courage and unlatch the door, but I couldn't. I was plain scairt.

I reached for the hatchet by the fireplace, and with my other hand touched the latch to make sure the bolt were throwed shut, but I'd never closed it when Pa and my brothers left.

I pushed against the rough plankin to hold the door tight closed and tried to work the bolt into the thick block of wood to hold it. No matter how hard I wiggled it I couldn't quite slip it into place. I leant against the planks and pressed my eye to the round knothole of daylight between the boards. A big golden eye stared back at me.

*No matter how scarce the victuals, share,
for you may be feeding angels unawares.*

I yanked open the door, and a raggedy girl in a dirty gray bandanna turned to run away. I grabbed her skinny saplin arm, the color of dark clover honey, and held on.

"Whoa!" I said. "What you doin out here?" I wanted to look at my hand to see if any of her color had rubbed off on me, but I kept my hand tight on her and stared hard into her wide golden-brown eyes, near the same color as her skin.

The girl, who looked to be about my age, glanced over my shoulder and peered into the kitchen. She acted like the fox I freed from one of Pa's leg traps last spring.

"Don't be scairt of me," I said. "Are you needin of somethin?"

"I'm hungry," she said, twistin at a piece of her torn skirt. "Cain't you spare me some pinders or cush?"

I looked past her and into the yard, where the chickens scratched at the bare ground. I couldn't let no one see me with her or they'd accuse me of bein a Negra-lovin John Browner.

"Where you from?" I asked. I weren't used to talkin to anyone her color out here. I tried to once when I was to the Janneys' mill in Waterford, but Pa gave me the back of his hand and told me that I weren't no better than "them."

"My family is out pickin for one of your neighbors down the road. I'm lost. I watched you workin this mornin and hoped you'd help me."

"Which family?" I asked, and wondered why she thought I'd help her. "Which family?" I asked again. We're all poorer than ashes in these parts, and I didn't know a one who could hire out their work.

"I cain't mind their names," she said as she studied at the ground, "but they live to the big white house with them tall posts. They traded for us to work in their fields."

I might not have got away from our farm much, but I couldn't remember ever seein such a house around here. I knowed that over Waterford way, where all the strange Quaker folk lived, the people my pa called slave lovers had houses bigger than ours, stone and brick where ours was split logs, but there wasn't any big white houses with posts on their porches.

The girl never looked at me. She just stood there and rubbed her dirty bare foot back and forth along the silvery floorboards of the porch.

What did I have that I could share with her? She looked to be even hungrier than me. I remembered the dried-out piece of corn bread in my pocket. My stomach complained again, but I pulled the corn bread out and offered it to her.

She grabbed the bread and stuffed the whole piece into her wide mouth.

"You're welcome," I said smart-like, and then in a nicer way, "Don't break your teeth. Sorry it's so hard, but it's about all I got here. Pa keeps a close watchin on our stores."

I glanced over my shoulder at the last of the scrapple stuck fast to the sides of the skillet. Pa would beat me if he knowed I shared anythin with anyone, especially some-one her color, but I couldn't let her go away without feedin her somethin more.

"C'mon in," I said, steppin outside to scoop up Mama's quilt. It flapped and lifted in the light wind like a bird's wing. "But if you hear my pa and brothers comin, you'll have to hightail it out that side door by the fireplace. You don't want to tangle with them."

She stepped through the doorway and looked around the room as though she wanted to memorize every crock, bench, and pan. I wished that I'd cleaned up a bit afore she come, but I couldn't hardly think of her as invited company.

"Not much here," I said, "but start to scrapin the skillet, and I'll try to find you somethin else." I spread Mama's quilt back onto my narrow bed, then patted the bench next to the table. The girl slid onto it and began to chip away at the burnt scrapple with a knife. Somehow she worked that knife around the skillet and watched every door and window. She reminded me of the white-faced owl in our barn. That big old moon-eyed bird seemed to spin its head nearly all the way round while it kept watch on me feedin the animals.

I could see that the girl were used to lookin out for herself, but she didn't know what bad trouble we'd be in if Pa or one of my brothers come home and found her here. I've always kept an ear cocked for their sounds, but now I strained even more for both our sakes. She needed to be out the side door and runnin into the woods afore they got close to the cabin or the dogs got wind of her.

"What's your name?" I asked, but afore she could answer, a sharp yippin cut through the quiet and the knife slipped from her hand and clanged to the floor. The girl stepped over the bench and headed for the side door, then stopped and turned back toward me. She reached out, grabbed my sleeve, then dropped it like it were an ember right out of the cookstove. She ran one way and then the other, the way a bobwhite does when a hawk passes over it.

Yip, yip, yip, whoooof, whooof, whooooo. The mixed

sounds of dogs runnin a hot trail come from somewhere behind the cabin.

"I cain't go out there," she sobbed. "They's too close. Them dogs smell me." Her eyes shone with tears. She laid wide her hands. They looked like pink flowers openin to the sun.

Out on the front porch steps, I heard the *clomp, clomp, clomp* of boots. Then the familiar *thump, thump, thump* as Pa knocked mud off his boots afore comin inside.

Dogs on one side of the cabin, Pa on the porch. We was treed like coons. I bent over the bench by our kitchen table and whispered to her, "Help me move this so's you can hide."

We slid the bench backward. I stuck my fingers into two small holes in the floor and lifted the cellar trapdoor. Cold air and the smells of damp earth, potatoes, apples, and smoked meat filled the kitchen.

"Hurry, and don't make no sound or we both be done for," I warned.

The girl stepped through the hole, backed down the steps, and disappeared into the darkness. I slid the trapdoor back over the openin and threw a handful of sand acrost the floor to hide our scuffle marks. Afore I had time to move the bench into place, Pa crossed the porch and pushed through the door.

*Never lay your broom bristles head-up
or you will find trouble just around the corner.*

Pa's big body blocked the bale of light on the floor. I kept
my head down and bent into my sweepin. I didn't dare
to stop workin, and I knowed that if I looked at him the
wrong way, he'd clout me.

"You," Pa said as he slammed the door shut behind
him. "You fetch up that scatter-gun and powder. We got
a runaway, and I can git me fifty dollars if I catch her afore
she leaves the county."

Her. Pa had said "her," and I knowed what that meant.
I forced myself not to look down at the trapdoor. I put my
hand to my mouth to stop a laugh from makin its way out.

Sometimes when I'm plain scairt or sad, I laugh. Sure to earn me the back of Pa's hand.

"Het it up!" Pa yelled. "Every man and hound from Purcellville to Hades is out lookin for her."

A fresh round of howlin and barkin jarred me into movin. The dogs whined, scratched at the door, and tried to push their way inside. From somewhere far off, I heard another pack of dogs yippin like they was runnin a bear.

I set my broom bristles down proper-like in the corner, climbed onto the stool in front of the stone fireplace, and stood on tiptoe to reach his shotgun—shiny, smooth, heavy, and cold, as cold as Pa's slatey eyes that squinted at me from acrost the room. I could feel them on my back.

"Grab the shot pouch and horn," Pa said. "They want her alive, but they don't say nothin about pickin buck and ball out of her dirty brown hide."

Grandpa's old shot pouch and powder horn hung from straps on a big iron hook in the mantel. I lifted them down and set them on the table as Pa brushed past me.

He started for the narrow ladder to the attic, turned, and said, "Put some victuals together for me."

"Oh law," I said under my breath. I'd have to go down to the cellar for some dried apples, jerky, and cracklins. I hadn't made any bread yet, and they was the only things I had to hand.

I waited for Pa to climb the ladder afore I picked up his victuals sack and lifted the door. I wondered how the girl felt, trapped down in that dark hole and hearin all the commotion just a few feet above her.

A clank and a dull thump sounded from below.

I poked my fingers into the trapdoor holes, lifted it, and leaned over the openin.

"Shhhhhhh," I hissed. "You get us both killt." I scuttled down the steps. "Keep quiet or we goin to end up like our old sow Daisy hangin from them hooks."

The girl set huddled in the dark amongst the near-empty barrels of potatoes and apples. She looked up at the meat swayin above her and rubbed the side of her head.

"We in trouble," I said. "They close on your trail. Why didn't you tell me?" She just set there and stared at me like I were speakin in tongues.

I moved past her and began to slide dried apple slices off a long thread of gut and into Pa's pouch. I stepped over to the wooden racks filled with strips of jerky and cracklins curled like pine shavins. I never gets to eat much of the meat I dry, but today I couldn't stop myself. First one piece and then another went into my mouth. I chewed quickly and swallowed so's Pa wouldn't smell it on me, then picked a wintergreen leaf out of my pocket and stuck it in my mouth.

The girl stood up and held out her hand. I passed her three small pieces, and she shoved one into her mouth. Then she pulled the dirty gray bandanna off her head, tucked two pieces inside it, and headed toward the ladder.

"Deer shot when it runs," I said.

"But the man say he gonna shoot me," she whispered.

I shook my head. "No, he ain't, not so long as you keep quiet."

The trouble girl turned back and crouched in the corner. She looked right wild.

An empty harvest basket set beside the steps. I picked some extra meat and apples, turnips and taters, and tucked them inside to fix for supper. I didn't want to have to make any more trips down into the cellar.

"You stick right where you are," I said, waggin my finger at her. I hooked the basket onto my arm, slung Pa's victuals sack over my shoulder, and climbed the steps. When I poked my head above the floor, I heard Pa movin acrost the attic.

"What you goin to do? Run out the door and into that pack of dogs?" I asked, but I didn't give her a chance to answer.

I climbed out, lowered the trapdoor into place, nudged the bench back over it, and set down the heavy basket.

Pa run into somethin, and it thudded onto the attic floor. A flood of bad words come from him. I grabbed my tin cup, gulped a mouthful of water, and scurried over to Pa's powder horn. He were backin halfway down the ladder when I unscrewed the plug and spit the water into the horn. There weren't no way he could shoot with his powder wet. Just as I replaced the cap, Pa's boot hit the kitchen floor.

*Dogs can see ghosts and will bark
when the ghosts are nearby.*

I handed Pa the horn and pouch. He looped the long straps around his neck, then looked round the messy kitchen. "What you been doin here all mornin? Don't you know how to work?" he asked as he jabbed the barrel of the gun into the center of my chest.

I didn't dare look at him or let him see he'd hurt me.

Pa picked up his victuals sack, walked out the door, and slammed it hard. From the small, hazy mica window, I watched as the dogs circled his legs like they hadn't seen him for days. The neighbor's hounds, who'd been sniffin all around the yard, turned and headed back toward the porch. I could hear him yellin at them. Tellin them to get off his farm (like they knowed this was his farm), and threatenin to shoot them if they didn't.

Pa walked acrost the yard with half a dozen dogs slinkin behind him, noses to the ground, tails down. Then they stopped, circled him, snuffled their noses into the soil and up into the air, like they was smellin fresh-killt deer. They turned and made a yelpin run for the porch again.

He picked up a water bucket, hurled it at the dogs, and promised to shoot them all. "Worthless!" he said, and yelled a string of words he usually saved up for me.

I watched till I couldn't see Pa or hear a dog barkin anywhere near. From somewhere in the woods, I heard the muffled sound of a shot. Close by, a raspy blue jay scolded, and a redbird hidden in some bushes called *purdy, purdy, purdy, purdy.*

I wondered where my brothers was. With my luck, *they* would come home too and expect me to fix up more victuals for the hunt. I were gettin tired of liftin up that door and worryin about all the things that was a tick away from goin wrong.

Two years ago, the last time Grandpa and me went to church afore he passed, the preacher told me that my "good common sense" kept me alive. My good common sense told me to go get that girl out of the cellar and out of my life, but my heart, the thing that gets in the way of my common sense, were tellin me somethin else.

"Mama, what should I do?" I asked. "Am I goin to get the beatin of my life tryin to help her?"

No answer.

"Mama, please, just give me a sign what to do."

No answer.

I wished that just this one time my mama could answer. That someone could tell me what were right and what were wrong. And why did I have to take a beatin for someone I didn't even know, or care about? Someone who probably wouldn't give me a butter bean if I were the hungry one. Why should I risk my own hide for her?

I quick-like righted the kitchen and picked up my big fanny basket but then set it back down. I wanted to go out and pick some tomaters and work around in the garden, but I needed to tell that whatever-her-name-was trouble girl that things was safe for now, so long as she stayed put and kept quiet. Why should I worry about easin her when I were nervous as a hen in a fox den? What did I care if she were scairt down there? I were gettin mad just thinkin about the fix she'd put me in.

I spun round, went straight to the bench, and clunked it on the floor as I moved it. Maybe put the scare into her, maybe so much of a scare she'd take off and head for the . . . the what?

I lifted the trapdoor just a sliver. I needed to make sure I could put things to rights if the boys surprised me.

"You in there?" I asked as I bent over the hole and squinted into the blackness.

"What you think?" she answered.

That made me mad. "Don't go smartin off, or you'll be sorry," I barked. Oh sweet Lord. I sounded like Pa.

I knelt down and leant forward. "You gonna have to stay quiet here till tomorrow mornin. You cain't go out yonder with all them hunters and dogs runnin the woods."

She snuffled loudly but didn't say a word.

"I'm goin to do some pickin and my chores, but I'm not goin to take any chances talkin to you again today," I said. "Don't cry. And don't you move and knock into anythin else. Understand?"

"Bless you," she whispered. Her words made me feel like the mud Pa had knocked off his boots.

I passed a crock of water and a tin cup down to her and let the door drop. I set on my haunches, rocked back and forth, back and forth, and tried to imagine how I would feel down there alone. Alone, in the dark, knowin that traders and slave catchers and packs of dogs was searchin the woods and fields for me.

I almost cried for her.

And then she sneezed.

I stomped on the floor, then knelt down till my lips almost touched the crack around the trapdoor. "One sneeze like that when everyone's to home, and you're dead. Dead like the possum Pa skinned last night." I glanced up at the window to make sure nobody were lookin in, then blew on the sand and watched my handprints disappear.

*Always carry a buckeye in your pocket
as a good-luck charm.*

I worked among the poles of greasy beans, tugged, twisted, and dropped the plumpin pods into my fanny basket. The beans was just startin to lose their green—I needed to string and hang 'em afore I missed my chance to make our winter supply of leather britches. I don't know why, but stringin and knottin those beans, well, it makes me feel like I'm settin my world to rights. I love hangin them beans on the back porch, line after line, like so many pairs of narrow green socks.

"Thank ya, beans, y'all be mighty good eatin," I sang to them. Then a layer of tomaters. "Thanks, all ya beauties. Y'all redder than a maple leaf." As I worked, I forgot all my worries, all my sorrows. The garden does that for me, makes me feel as healt up as the arnica and comfrey poultices the preacher's wife made for me once after I angered my pa.

From the field nearby, I heard the sweet slurried song of the lark. I answered with my own whistlin song. He were confused, sang right back, and I whistled again and smiled. I'm a right good whistler but most never do it in front of anyone.

All around me the barn swallows wove and dipped, chittered and dived. Under the eaves of the shed, their mud nests overflowed with gape-mouthed babies beggin for their suppers. A phoebe, tail dippin up and down like the handle on our water pump, left his perch and snapped a moth out of the air in front of me.

Maybe I were feelin too good, too right with things, but the next minute I looked up and there she stood in the doorway. Her brown hair stuck out in tufts like the pinfeathers on the baby swallows. The dirty gray bandanna in her hand bulged with a passel of Pa's victuals. She took one look at me and started to jump off the porch and hightail it.

"Stop!" I shouted, and ran toward her. "You cain't run when they's so close to you. Them dogs'll catch your scent."

She turned toward me and her golden eyes looked big as

chestnuts. Her mouth hung slack open, and she gasped for each breath like the little doe the dogs run down and cornered by the woodshed. I could feel how scairt she were.

But could she feel how scairt *I* were? What if she got caught and told where she'd been hidin? What if afore I could get indoors and make things aright, Pa or my brothers come in and seen the cellar all tore apart? And what if she got shot, and hurt, and sent back . . . sent back where?

Boom. I dropped my gatherin basket, and the birds tornadoed around me. A shattered, bloody nest laid at my feet. A barn swallow swooped past, skimmed just inches above the ground, and arced up to the spot where the nest once clung. As it flew, it made a keenin cry—most the saddest sound ever.

I could hear my brothers laughin, but I couldn't see them. Another shot, another nest on the ground. When I looked over to the porch, that trouble girl had disappeared. I reached into my apron pocket to rub against the reassurin smooth of my good-luck buckeye, but it weren't there.

*Kill a swallow
and bad luck will follow.*

My heart felt near broke for the swallows, but I were fearin for myself and for the girl. Clem yelled that he needed food for his hunt. Samuel whistled for his cry of dogs, and they streamed into the barnyard from three sides. I didn't see how they'd missed that girl.

I grabbed the handle of my basket, heavy with tomaters—some of them ripe ones squished from the fall—and run for the porch. I needed to make sure that the trapdoor were closed afore the boys got into the cabin.

The door stood ajar. I pushed it wider and ran inside. On the floor, a little pile of jerky spilled from the girl's gray bandanna. The trapdoor gaped open, the bench laid on its side, and two disks of dried apple stared up from the floor.

Bathsheba and Delia was close at my heels. I whirled on them. "Stay, girls. Tend to your manners," I scolded, and they almost stopped, but they caught the smell of the jerky and near trampled me gettin to it.

I could hear them boys behind me. They clomped up the steps. The dogs tore at the bandanna. I run to the trapdoor, and there, framed in the dim square of light on the ladder, the girl backed down into the cellar. I dropped the door into place, righted the bench, scooped up the bandanna, and stuffed it into my basket of tomaters.

"Girl!" Clem yelled. "Look at that mess of spoilt maters." He pointed at them. He grabbed me by the neck, bent me over the basket, and shoved my face hard into the pile. I sputtered, pushed myself up, and used the sides of my balled fists to rub the burnin juice out of my eyes.

"And you let them dogs in. You know them dogs don't come inside."

I guessed I couldn't explain that they wasn't hardly invited in.

Bathsheba yelped as Clem's heavy boot landed in her soft flank. She usually outruns everything, but her long, saggin teats slowed her some. Afore Clem could reach Delia, both hounds was out the door. I wished I could foller them. I knowed that them killt swallows was bringin in bad, bad luck for me.

"Get us some pack food," Samuel ordered. "We gonna be out trackin upriver all night."

I pushed strands of wet hair behind my ears, blinked my blurry, burnin eyes, and started for the basket of victuals I had set beside the trapdoor. Samuel spied the two golden disks of apple a second afore I could kick them acrost the floor and out of sight.

"You been in them cellar apples?" he yelled. He walked toward the trapdoor, picked up the basket of food, and kicked the bench over and out of the way. Then he stuck his fingers in the door holes and threw it open. Afore I could duck or move out of Samuel's way, he walloped me.

*If you hear whispering, it is the sperrits
arguing which one is going to be near you
for the day and night.*

My arm and shoulder was on fire. The stabbin pains
shot through me till my stomach churned. I turned my
head and throwed up, then Mama's fingers brushed over
me softly, like moth wings, and I heard her a-whisperin to
me. I didn't want to move. I didn't want Mama's touch or
voice to go away.

I opened my eyes, but all I saw were black. Black as the
bat cave over to the river. But the smell here, the smell
in this black, were a mix of apples, smoke, earth, my
throwed-up bitter waters, and none of the stink of the bat
cave.

I moaned and tried to sit up, but a rough hand pushed

me down and covered my mouth. A voice whispered in my ear, "Shhhhh."

"Am I dead?" I asked. Was the sperrits arguin over me?

"You be dead if you don't stop talkin. Let them git out the cabin," the voice whispered.

The voice. I remembered the girl comin out of the cabin. The shots, the bird nests all blowed up, the girl, that trouble girl, were the one who caused all this, and it were her voice talkin to me now.

I laid still but couldn't stop shakin. The girl's hand took ahold of mine and gently squeezed and patted it. Hot tears spilled down the side of my face and onto the hard-packed dirt floor.

Just a few feet above my head I heard the shufflin and clompin of boots, the thunk of somethin hittin the floor, and then the familiar sound of the heavy oak door slammin shut. Nothin but the creakin of floorboards settlin back into place—and then nothin.

"You, girl, you got a mess a trouble in your life too," she whispered. "I thought I were worst off to anyone, but you got it bad." Her hand patted at me, then rested on my good arm.

"Are you pityin me?" I asked. I pulled my arm out from under her hand and moved a few inches away.

I don't know how long I slept, but when I woke, I felt the scratchy warmth of a feed sack laid over me and heard the soft, low sounds of her hummin nearby. I tried turnin onto my other side, but the pain kept me still.

"What we gonna do now?" I asked.

The girl stopped hummin and turned over toward me. I could feel her breath on my face.

"We goin to get away from here afore you . . . we get killt," she said.

I felt about near as killt now as I ever had.

"Did you hear where they be lookin for me? Did you see the way your pa went when he left?"

Samuel's words, "trackin upriver," run through my mind. "North along the river, but they could be anywhere the dogs lead them." I groaned as I tried to move into a comfortable position.

"North where I'm goin," she said. "Follerin the North Star now for all the nights since I run."

She started talkin at me, soft-like, tellin me a story, but tellin herself the story too.

"My ma and papa, they gone now," she said. "Ma sold and sent away south; Papa sold and sent I don't know where. Last time I saw him his arms was tied behind. He had a bit in his mouth, his lips curled back like he smilin, but the blood drippin from his mouth and runnin down him. And my baby sister, I can still hear her cryin, and my ma screamin when the soul-driver man pull Promise out of her arms. He tell Ma that she never see her baby or me again."

She paused. The colors of her story faded, then brighted as she talked. "Why don' they sell us together the way they say they goin do? He shove my baby sister into a wagon full a people. People she don't know."

I felt the girl shudder next to me.

"I tried to run after my Promise." Her voice caught as she continued. "But the man hit me over and over, knock me down, and throw me into his wagon. He thinks I am hurt some bad, so he don't chain me. Soon as I could move, I slip over the side of the wagon and hide all day in a ditch. I want my ma and papa, my baby sister, but they gone. I do what my ma always told me, I foller where the Drinkin Gourd points to the North Star."

Even through the darkness I could see everythin. The cart crammed full of people chained together, the little girl cryin, lookin for her sister's face and listenin for the sound of her ma or pa's voice. Her sorrow made me forget about mine.

"I turned round, seen Promise's wagon leavin. She were holdin out her hands, reachin for me, but I"—she gulped—"I hurt so bad I cain't move, and all I do is watch her till I cain't hear nothin or see her no more."

This time I reached out and found her hand. I couldn't imagine havin a mama and papa, and a baby sister I loved and who loved me, but even worse, I couldn't imagine losin them.

*Make sure nobody follows you
and walks in your tracks, or you will die.*

I slept again and woke to the sound of a purrin snore beside me. I reached out to smooth Bathsheba's sleek fur, but my hands met tufts of wiry hair.

I weren't in the barn with a sleepin dog. I were in the cellar, trapped, with the runaway girl who started up my problems. If it hadn't been for her, I'd be back out in the garden pickin tomaters, or shovelin our cow Hildie's dung out of the barn. Anythin would be better than where I were now.

I slowly pushed myself up, winced with pain, then touched my arm, my shoulder, and my wrist. "No bones stickin out anywhere," I said aloud, "but I am right hurt."

I couldn't see the girl, but I felt the rough sack slip off as she rolled over.

"We best be gettin out of here afore them men come back," she said. "Only the good Lord knows how long we been down here."

We? "We best be gettin out of here"? Just what I needed. Not bad enough that I'm a mite smaller than most girls, and that my ugly red hair stands out like broom corn, but now look what I were stuck with—a tall, raggedy runaway slave girl who dragged trouble behind her like a tail. We'd stick out worse 'n chickens in Sunday dresses.

"Who says you're goin anywhere nearst to where I'm goin?" I asked.

"You. You's the one who say 'what *we* gonna do.' "

I thought back on those words. I had said that. Maybe I were just plumb scairt at the time and not thinkin right, but here I were down in a cellar hole, all beat up, and talkin about runnin away with someone I'd never even seen till today.

"I don't know where you gonna go," I said quietly, "but I cain't stay round for any more beatins from anyone. I have to run while I can, and I don't need no one follerin me."

Oh, I felt right sorry for that girl. I felt sorry down to my toes, but I'd gotten deep in trouble for her, and even though I knowed she'd lost everythin, well, I had to look out for myself now.

I bit down on my lip as I pushed myself up from the

hard-packed dirt floor. Every inch of me hurt, but I couldn't stop to think on that. I waited for a sound, any sound above me. Nothin moved, nothin creaked. I raised the trapdoor slightly and ducked my head as the sand from the floor sifted down and onto my hair. I pushed the door open wider, stepped up, and poked my head over the edge.

The last rosy light of the day made the cabin glow. I loved this time when I were home alone and all peaceful-like. I'd sit out on the porch steps when Pa and my brothers wasn't around, maybe Bathsheba or Delia beside me, and watch the sun settin and listen to all them birds callin one to another as they found their way back to their homes.

From outside, I heard the shrill talkin of the nighthawks as they began to crisscross the sky above the clearin. *Beanzz, beanzz, beanzz,* they cried.

"Beans is right," I said as I looked down at the girl. "We best be loadin up on food. Jerky, cracklins, whatever we can fit in these sacks easy-like." I turned and stepped back down into the cellar.

She bent, picked up a bag, and began stuffin it with taters. "No," I said. "Load it with jerky, cracklins, dried apple slices, apples, anythin you can carry easy, not them heavy taters."

She nodded, dumped most of the taters on the floor, and reached for the meat.

I slowly loaded a bundle, then slipped on the shoulder sling I carry when I'm pickin apples. From the racks below the smoked ham, I gathered up some soup bones, a hunk of smoked ham, and a fat pig's knuckle. I tied the sling closed as best I could with my hurt arm.

That trouble girl were lookin at me and shakin her head. "Ummm, ummm, what you doin with them? Goin make us some soup or jelly us some knuckles when we runnin?"

She was sayin "we" again. "Don't you sass me, trouble girl. I know what I'm doin."

I climbed the steps first. Slowly, slowly, and wincin for the pain I felt along my side and shoulder. The bundle and sling of food seemed near heavy as them big rocks I hauled for the garden wall. I pulled myself up and sprawled acrost the floor but left my feet danglin over the cellar hole.

"You gots to move," she said as she pushed her bag of food through the openin. I rolled over on my good side and crawled away from the cellar. She stepped out of the hole, grabbed her bag, and looked around the cabin.

I set up. "We need to close the trapdoor." Slow and quiet-like, we dropped it into place. From habit, I looked for the bench to move it back into its spot over the door, but the bench laid on its side, exactly where Samuel had kicked it.

"With a little luck, they won't come back tonight," I said. "Give us a few hours of start on them while they're trackin you upriver."

We hoisted the sacks over our shoulders, and I tightened the knot on my sling. I looked around the cabin and waited for scairt or sad to fill me, but it didn't. I just needed to get out, and fast. One last look around. Were there anythin else I needed?

Acrost the room on the dry sink, I saw the carved handle of my grandpa's huntin knife. Pa must've set it down when he come home for food. I limped over, picked up the knife, and stuck it into one of the apples in my sling. The girl disappeared out the door. I felt her feet drummin acrost the porch. With luck, maybe we'd lose each other, but then, I weren't feelin too lucky today.

I started to foller her, but stopped. If I stayed here, I'd go on barely livin and bein as nameless as the kittens Pa drowned over to the crick. Well, I were near to growed up now, I knowed my way round the woods, and I could make a livin somehow, somewhere far away. Uh-huh, near to growed up now. I looked around the room and saw some bright squares of blue, red, and green patchwork next by my pillow. I shifted my load, walked over to my bed, and tugged out my old rag doll. "Here we go, Hannah girl," I said, tuckin her inside my sling. "I couldn't no more forget you than my mama and grandpa."

When you're running from enemies,
never look over your shoulder
or their bad luck will snare you.

I crost the porch and went down the rickety steps, then made my way through the barnyard. A few things needed doin afore I left. My grandpa had taught me how to tend his beehives and harvest the honey, but he had also cautioned me to always tell the bees of any great happenins. I picked up my bee stick and walked over to the bench line of log gum hives where the stragglers, the last of the hardworkin bees, was findin their way home for the night.

Tap, tap, tap, the stick moved from log to log to log. "I'm leavin here, all you good bees. I'm leavin here and all the bad times. Forever. I'll miss you," I said.

I moved away from the hummin log gums, said a fare-thee-well to my tidy little garden and to the last of the hens headin in to roost.

I passed my little square of tomaters. There, lyin on the ground, lookin up at me sure as the buck's eye it were called after, were my good-luck charm. I picked it up, felt at its smooth, then slipped it into my pocket. I'd be needin all the luck I could find.

Grandpa's two old workhorses, Delilah and Samson, hung their heads over the crooked-rail fence between the pasture and the barnyard. I stroked the blaze on Delilah and smoothed Samson's forelock, all the while thankin them for the hard work and good comfort they always give me. Delilah whinnied when I reached into my sack and pulled out two apples for them. I always spoilt them, just like Grandpa did, but who would spoil them now?

Afore I left, I had one last thing to do. I stopped by the side of the cabin, picked a handful of the pink roses planted by my mama's own hand, and carried them over to the little buryin ground I'd tended since Grandpa passed.

Small wooden markers had the carved names of brothers and sisters I'd never met. Next come my mama—Hannah Cullen Nicoll, and Aaron E. Cullen, my dear grandpa. I knelt down and tucked tiny pink buds near the graves of my brothers and sisters, and a handful of the sweet-smellin roses atop Mama's and Grandpa's markers for the last time.

"Good-bye, Mama. Good-bye, Grandpa. Won't you

stay by my side?" I asked as I turned and walked into the comin night.

Dozens of tiny bats weaved through the darkenin sky and flitted past me. I knowed that it were just an old tale about them catchin in your hair, but I couldn't help shirkin from them. I ducked my head, hunched my shoulders under the weight of the bags, and limped along the trail above the crick.

When I found the narrow path that led from the bank through the brambles and poison ivy, I slipped and slid all the way down. Them thorns tore at me like cat claws and rooster beaks. The poison ivy never bothers me none, nary an itch nor a bump when I hold it, but the brambles— they hurt somethin fierce. I had to bite at my lips to keep from cryin out.

When I finally got to the water, I waded till my feet sank into the mud and disappeared. I stopped, crouched, and splashed my face and arms. Then I drank its cool sweetness from my cupped hands. I could've stayed there forever, the water runnin over me and soothin my torn arms, but I made myself get up and keep movin. I could feel the smooth pebbles and the suck and pull of the mud as I walked along the crick bed and headed south. My guess was that Pa and my brothers had probably headed north up top along the sycamore trail. By now, they'd be takin another track as they searched for the girl. Too bad for her if she went the wrong way and ran into them, but good for me.

I felt bad thinkin like that.

The moon, her horns pointin to the east, were waxin fair and clear. I could see ahead along a goodly piece of the water that stretched in front of me like a wide silver ribbon. From the edge of the crick, the big rocks, the ones I loved to play on, loomed dark-like and not near as friendly-lookin as they was by day. My heart pounded and I glanced quick side to side, searchin for anythin movin along the bank. The noise of the runnin water wrapped round me, hidin my sounds, but also hidin the sounds of anyone passin nearby. I stopped myself from lookin back over my shoulder; I didn't want to court no trouble.

*If you want to get rid of a ghost,
make the sign of the cross, spit, and dare
the ghost to come out or leave for good.*

I hurt somethin bad, but I walked most of the hot, thick
night, switchin my sling and sack from side to side. I had
plenty of time to think about things, like how mad Pa and
my brothers would be when they got to home and didn't
have any food waitin for them. First they'd be yellin for
me, but once they lifted the trapdoor and found both me
and their stores missin, they'd be spittin mad and kickin
at everythin in the room. This time it wouldn't be me
feelin their boots.

I wanted to whistle. Whistlin in the dark usually made
me feel safe, but tonight I weren't goin to feel safe no matter. I were fine walkin in the bright water. And fine so long

as I saw the stars and the shinin light of the moon, but sometimes the trees touched from one side of the bank to the other and made a long dark tunnel. When I stepped into the blackness, I traced an X in the air, then spit to keep away the sperrits. Then I'd come out of the tunnel and into the silvery world again and walk, walk, walk through deep cold water up to my knees, and sometimes through shallow warm water most as gentle on me as a spring rain.

I reached my good hand through the hole in the sling, pulled out an apple, and chewed it through, even the core and the bitter of the seeds. Ahead of me there were another long stretch of trees archin over the crick and makin the black water look like it run into a cave.

I tried to move my packs to ease my hurtin, but what I really needed were rest. Just a short nap. I wouldn't dare to sleep for fear of wastin too much time. I walked on a little farther; then the crick made a wide, easy sweep, and the current slowed till it sounded like it were murmurin to me.

I walked through the water till I reached the spot where it rested quiet against a cut in the bank. The sandy shore blanketed with leaves looked to be about as good a bed as I'd ever find. Around me, the sounds of crickets and the *whippoorwill, whippoorwill, whippoorwill* voice of the goatsucker bird made me feel safe. He'd call till almost daylight but would stop if anyone passed nearby.

I shrugged out of the sling, dropped the sack on the

ground, and used my feet to smooth a sandy place for a few minutes of nappin. Then I crouched on all fours, plumped the sling for a pillow, laid down, and shut my eyes.

I thought about that girl again, and a picture of her scairt face come into my head and wouldn't leave. She didn't know these woods and hideouts like I did, but what did I care? I hoped that I'd never see her again. Last thing I remembered were sayin to myself, "I'm better off without her."

The voice is what woke me. It whispered low, "Don't move." I laid still, opened my eyes, squinted against the sun that slanted through the trees. I thought I'd been dreamin that voice. Then I heard it again. "Don't move," it said, and my eyes was open so's I knowed I weren't sleepin. I wanted to turn my head, find who were speakin, but the voice warned again, "Stay still."

The smell of crushed sycamore leaves and the soft scrunchin sound of feet walkin acrost them let me know that someone were gettin closer. My heart thudded. I wanted to push up and run, but I felt froze to the ground.

A shadow moved between me and the sun. That trouble girl stood over me holdin a big branch. I opened my eyes wide and looked into hers. She tilted her head toward me and gave it a slow shake, like she were sad to do what she were goin to do. She lifted the branch above her afore I could move. I closed my eyes and yelled.

*If you want fair weather after you
kill a snake, you must bury it.*

A bare foot nudged me, then rolled me over like a log. "What you mean yellin like that?" the trouble girl asked. "Folks must've heard you clear to town."

I set up, held my hands against my heart to keep it from burstin through my skin, and brushed the leaves out of my hair. The branch laid on the ground a few inches from me. Stickin out from underneath it were the rusty brown body of a copperhead snake, its mouth wide open, fangs down, and its mean cat eyes starin right at me. I must've slept next to that snake all night.

The girl stuck out her hand to help me up. I stood, all wobbly and shakin, and we looked at each other eye to eye. I didn't want to have to say it, but I did. "Thank you for savin me."

"Now we don't owe each other nothin," she answered.

But I felt like now I did owe her somethin, and I wouldn't never forget it. I stuck out my hand and took hers again. "Looks like we're spost to be together," I said. "Let's eat a few bites, then get movin up the crick."

We both set on a big limb that stretched like a bridge over the water. We opened our sacks, pulled out some apple slices and jerky, and chewed in silence. Soon we both be swingin our legs and talkin, almost forgettin for a few minutes where we was and why we was runnin.

"What your name?" the girl asked me.

"I don't have no name. My mama died just when I were borned and nobody bothered to give me one, ceptin Grandpa, who always called me Sweet Girl when we were alone. But you can call me Girl like everyone else does."

"Girl ain't no name for you. I never knowed someone with no name. Even the Nkanga hens on the plantation has themselves names," she said to me as she stood up and walked back acrost the limb and onto the bank.

"I give you one, but I needs to find a name that fits you good." She bent to knot the end of the sack, then swung it over her shoulder.

I shuffled acrost the limb, climbed off, slipped my achin arm through the loop of the sling, then tied my bag closed.

"What's your name?" I asked her, but she were on the other side of the clearin and hadn't heard me.

"Hey, girl," I shouted, "what you doin there?"

She kicked soil and leaves over the long, patterned body of the copperhead.

"Hopin for fair weather," she said. "Cain't leave this snake without a buryin or we have storms."

The girl finished coverin the snake and stepped off the bank and into the crick. We both kicked and threw handfuls of water onto my sleepin spot and everywhere our feet had touched the ground.

I started to ask her name again, but the words never left my mouth. Loud barkin come from somewhere down to the bottoms. I could hear bayin and buglin, the song the hounds sing when they on a warm trail. Then more bayin, and this time too close. Was they pickin up our smells?

"We in trouble," I said. "Let's get movin. Stay in the crick."

She looked at me and nodded afore she took off through the water. I follered close behind her, makin too much noise, splashin, slippin, and fallin over rocks and branches. I felt like I couldn't raise my feet up another step.

This part of the crick twisted and turned, all crooked every which way. We'd go one way for a few minutes and near meet ourselves goin the other. It felt like we was makin no gains.

Then things started lookin like I'd seen them afore. We was in the Horseshoe Bends near to Bush Crick where Pa brought his wheat to be milled.

We come to a split. Wide waters one way, the other a

narrow run I thought to be Bush Crick. We stood at the whirlin pool where the two met and looked up one and down the other. "Which way?" the trouble girl asked me, but I didn't have no answer.

Bathsheba, my favorite of Pa's dogs, howled out her familiar yodel-like call from somewhere close by, and we took off runnin down the shinbone of water that rushed ahead of us.

*Finding a warm piece of wood from a tree struck
by lightning will bring you great powers.*

The girl and me didn't stop. We sloshed through the water not sayin a word. My sacks pounded up and down against my back and hurt shoulder as I run.

We kept runnin till Bathsheba's bayin sounded a county away. I knowed that the old hound must be right confused, smellin my scent out where it didn't belong.

The girl stopped runnin for a minute, bent over, her hands on her knees, and panted. Sweat dripped off her and into the fast-movin water. She straightened, clutched at her side, and bent over again.

"You hurtin?" I asked. She nodded and stayed bowed

like an old woman. I walked over to her, put my hand on her shoulder, and said, "Let's stop. Let's drink some water and rest a few minutes."

The girl backed over to a big flat rock in the middle of the crick and dropped her sack. I follered and dropped my bag and sling beside hers. We both knelt, cupped our hands, and drank till we couldn't drink no more.

The heaviness of the day were takin all the life out of us. We was both drippin wet, our clothes stickin to us, and every breath hard-like. I splashed water all over myself and then onto her. She turned toward me, laughin, and slapped the water hard till I were wet through.

Once, on a day near as hot as today, my grandpa told me that even a fish would be sufferin. I looked down at the small streaks of silver minnows dartin from shadow to shadow in the crick. They didn't look to be sufferin none. I wished I could be one of them for just a few minutes.

The girl straightened, walked through the water, and climbed onto another big rock. I joined her, hauled up, and we set together back to back, our knees tented in front of us, the water rushin and whirlin around us.

"What's your name?" I asked over my shoulder.

"Zenobia," she said.

"What kind of name is that?"

"Zenobia is my gramma's name, and Zenobia were a queen."

The girl pushed back her thick, dark hair and shook the

sweat off her face. "Zenobia my milk name, and Ma say if I don't like it when I get old enough I can change it. But I like it."

"Zenobia," I said aloud. "Zenobia." I rolled it around in my mouth like a smooth stone. "Come on, Zenobia, we got more travelin to do."

We stood up together, walked over to the flat rock, and picked up our sacks. We was soggy to the bone. The wind turned and carried the distant sound of the barkin and howlin of the hounds. And then a deeper sound and a long rollin rumble like the earth were goin to split open.

Another rumble; then the wind started tearin at the trees till their leaves whirled through the air. Then a crack, like someone firin at us, and a clap of thunder louder and closer than any I'd ever heard.

"Guess you didn't bury that old snake good enough!" I yelled to Zenobia.

Ahead of us a huge sycamore tree, its heart burnt out of it from the lightnin strike, stood smolderin.

Zenobia took off and run toward the tree. I shouted a warnin to her about takin cover. She reached the blackened tree and peeled a short piece of the charred bark from its edge.

"This lightnin wood save us," she said as she broke the sliver in half and handed a still-warm piece to me. "Keep it for good luck."

I didn't want to pass up any chance of good luck. I

tucked the sliver into my sack, and we raced for a sheltered openin in the rocks.

We smelt the rain afore it hit. Then it come down so hard and loud it wiped out the sounds of the crick.

Zenobia reached the openin afore me. "It's a cave," she yelled over her shoulder. She shouted somethin else, but her voice were lost in the wind and rain.

I ran and almost made it to the openin when a lightnin strike hit so close I heard a sizzlin sound, like fritters fryin in grease. Right with it come the thunder, ear-burstin loud. I ducked my head, and Zenobia's hand yanked me inside just as a young cottonwood crashed acrost the willows and sealed the entry hole closed.

*A whistlin girl and a crowin hen
always come to some bad end.*

I heard Zenobia pantin, but I couldn't see her. I twisted round and looked back at the openin, all covered now by a crisscross of branches. I felt like I were lookin out of one of my willow baskets.

"We be trapped," I said as I shifted my bundle and sling and turned back toward Zenobia. Slowly my eyes got used to the darkness, and I could see her face peerin over the top of the bundle.

"Trapped feel good and safe," she said.

"Trapped never good," I answered. It give me the all-overs when I thought back to the animals I'd seen strugglin to free themselves from Pa's lines, workin so hard they'd gnaw off their own legs to get free. "Right now we need to rest, and then we'll break through them branches and get out of here. Best travelin by night anyways." I shivered and drew my wet pack up against my body.

The floor of the cave were covered with twigs, leaves, and bits and pieces of fish bones and crawdad. It smelt thick, musky, like where the river otters rubbed and rolled on the banks of Catoctin Crick. I didn't even want to think on what else were in the cave.

Zenobia's pantin quieted; then she settled into a purrin sleep. I were beginnin to think that she could drop off anywhere. My heart calmed. Some people are afeared of bein closed into dark or small places, but somehow they always made me feel safe. I liked it when I could see folk but they couldn't see me. But bein trapped in here made me feel right rattled. I closed my eyes. The sounds of the crick and the rain stutterin onto the leaves of the fallen cottonwood seeped into me.

Here I were, trapped in a cave with a runaway slave girl. A few days ago I'd been trapped in another way. Trapped at the cabin with Pa and my brothers and never a hope of much good happenin to me. Now, I were on my way, but on my way to where and what?

We both slept. Zenobia woke first and called to me. "Girl. Listen."

I didn't need her to tell me to listen. I heard dogs barkin, their yelps piercin right through the roarin of the water. Then I felt heavy feet thuddin along the sandy banks above us, and then the crashin sounds of someone slippin down the bank and through the brush. Then a loud splash and yellin.

"Bank fall in!" a familiar voice yelled. "And them fool dogs. Where they go?"

I could see movement through the tree branches and the flash of Pa's red shirt. My heart took a jump. More yellin and then the sound of Pa workin his way up the cliff and through the brush. Finally, just the sound of the river roarin past us.

I gulped air, Zenobia exhaled, and then the frenzied sounds of a pack of huntin dogs slidin down the bank and thrashin through the stream. They howled, barked, and lunged into the branches that laid acrost the openin to the cave.

"We done for," Zenobia said.

I figured it wouldn't take more 'n a few minutes for the trackers to circle back to us once they heard the familiar findin calls of the hounds. Their barks was so loud I couldn't hardly think.

"Zenobia!" I shouted. "Start breakin a hole in them branches so's I can reach my hand through."

For once she didn't ask me no questions, but she looked at me like I were a crazy girl. The cave were so small she could barely squirm past, but soon I could smell green and hear the *snap, crack, snap* of twigs as she broke them and tossed the pieces aside.

The dogs yipped and barked as they pawed at the fallen

tree. Two or three of the hounds fought each other till one yelped and cried out in pain.

I rolled onto my good side and curled up like a fiddlehead so's I could turn around and wriggle toward Zenobia and the little circle of light. The bundle and sling got in my way. They snagged on tree roots and slid off my shoulders, but I tugged at them and slipped them back on. I couldn't leave our food and Hannah doll behind.

"Move," I said. She looked back at me, nodded, tore at one last handful of twigs, and pushed herself against the side of the cave.

Zenobia had made an openin the size of a fox's hole. One of the dogs found the hole and worked his head into it. He snarled, teeth bared, as he lunged, pushed, and lunged again, all the while tryin to force his way into the cave.

I slid the packs off my back, reached inside the sling, and grabbed some ham bones and a knuckle. I used one of the big knobs of bone to push the dog back from the hole, and then I opened my hand flat so's he could grab the bone without bitin me. His mouth clamped over the bone; he backed out of the hole and disappeared. Another head poked inside the openin, this one whinin to get at me. Another bone snatched from my hand, and another, and another till each one of the five greedy hounds, not wantin to share with the others, slunk off to worry their bones in peace. I waited, expectin to hear the men shoutin to the dogs, or worse yet, lookin for us. What if the dogs carried them bones back to the trail? But no, I know hounds, and they loves a hunt, but once they get a bone they'll hide out till it is eat to nothin.

Outside, there weren't a sound to be heard exceptin for the crick. I reached past the bag of food and grasped Zenobia's fingers. She curled them round mine, and we held on to each other.

I don't know how much time passed, but the quiet stayed and slivers of peachy light shone through the cottonwood's leaves.

"It looks to be clearin out there and sun be settin," I said.

Zenobia lifted her head and glanced toward the openin. "I cain't hear no more hounds."

"We safe for now," I said. "Let's eat a few bites and think on what we goin to do."

I cupped my hand to my ear and heard the sound of a kingfisher bird rattlin like a bucket of dried butter beans. That bird wouldn't never stay close if anyone come nearby us.

I fumbled around inside my sack, felt for the soft rounds of apple, the jerky, and cracklins, and pulled them out. I stuffed a sweet apple slice into my mouth and chewed, then bit into a tough piece of jerky and tugged at its stubbornness.

Last night had been a fattenin moon. We could wait awhile afore leavin the cave and we'd still have plenty of light for travelin.

"Girl," Zenobia said. "What we goin to do?"

The "we" in her question didn't bother me none now.

"Finishin our food so's we can get out of here," I said.

I heard her chompin and felt her movin her bag. She wriggled sideways, then propped her face on her hands.

"I were watchin from the porch when you was workin and pickin out in your tomater patch. You was whistlin like that yeller bird on the fence post. You whistle to him; he whistle right back to you; you sound jus' like him."

"I'm a right fine whistler," I admitted, glad that someone had noticed somethin good about me.

Zenobia's finger poked into my shoulder. "What were that bird you was singin to?"

"That were a lark," I answered.

"I be thinkin on that and now I namin you Lark, and that ain't a milk name, that a name you keep. You Lark."

"Lark," I said, "I likes that name Lark," and I whistled its sweet flutin song for her. We both giggled, but then I shuddered. I remembered one of the last times Pa let me go to school. My teacher caught me whistlin, and she said, "Miss Nicoll, whistlin girls and crowin hens always come to some bad end." I wouldn't let myself come to no bad end.

I looked over my shoulder. The light were beginnin to fade. I dug my toes in the sand to gain purchase, then wiggled backward a few feet toward the openin. Then I realized that my toes was wet, covered with cold runnin water that had crept up from the risin crick and into the cave.

"Mama, Grandpa, don't let us come to no bad end."

Then I yelled, "Zenobia! We in trouble. The water's risin fast. Either we get ourselfs out now or we gonna drown."

*Make a heartfelt wish when you see the first star come out,
and your wish will come to pass.*

Zenobia crouched by the openin and tore at the branches. I slipped next to her and pulled off the stubborn twigs till we could grab the trunk. The water rose quick—one second an inch deep, the next over our feet and climbin fast.

We pushed against the trunk, rocked it back and forth, and pushed again till the tree groaned, slipped sideways, and rolled into the torrent.

I looked down at my hands. They ran with ribbons of blood. I shook them and reached out to dunk them in the risin water, but Zenobia yelled at me to get out.

"We don't have no time to waste!" she shouted.

I looked over at her and saw that she were bloodied too. "Lark, you go. I pass you the sacks."

I crawled out of the flooded cave and tried to reach for our sacks, but the water picked me up like a leaf boat and whisked me downstream. Small branches whipped acrost my cheeks, tore at my forehead, and caught in my hair. My hands, knees, and legs slammed into boulders, but I couldn't take no time to think of the hurtin. I gulped water, gasped at the air, paddled like my Delia dog, and fought to keep my head above the powerful current.

The water slowed and smoothed. I half floated, half paddled, and worked my way toward the bankside. I almost made it, but another crick, this one narrower, rain-swolled, and flowin as fast as any I'd ever seen, hit me broadside and twirled me round and round. I paddled but didn't make an inch of headway. I spun and spun, down into the dark waters, sputterin and chokin and all the time thinkin to myself that I weren't goin to let this be my end.

I grabbed for a branch afore it washed past me and held on with both hands. I kicked hard and the branch shot straight up and out of the twirlin waters, then bore me along. Off to my side, I saw a light patch of sand juttin out like a long, white finger. I held on, turned toward the landfall, kicked hard, and my foot finally scumbled against the gravelly bottom so's I could push myself onto shore.

I laid there on the sand, pantin and feelin every bit of

me hurtin now. "Mama," I said, "I didn't think things could get any worst."

"What you didn't think to be worst?" asked Zenobia, who stood on the bank just a few feet above me. She were near dry, and our food sacks on her shoulders looked to be in fine shape.

"You went heels over," she said, and laughed. "I held on to them tree roots and climb along the bank."

Her humor made me mad. "Look at me. A fine thing for you to laugh at me all bloody and hurt."

Zenobia grinned. "You be alive; you not be broken; you not be caught." She scrambled down the bank and reached for my hand. I didn't want her help, but I looked up at her, grasped her tightly, and let her pull me up. My legs wobbled like a newborn filly's.

"We need to get back in the crick so's they cain't pick up our scent," I said to her, actin like nothin special happened to me and like I were the boss of both of us. I reached for my sling and sack, which I didn't want to carry, and slipped them onto my achin shoulders.

"My buckeye!" I said, pattin at my pocket. "Oh, thank the good Lord, my buckeye is safe."

"Why you worryin now about a buckeye?" Zenobia asked.

"It's my good luck," I said. "My grandpa give it over to me. He always carried it; now I always has it in my pocket. I'd never let go of it for nothin."

Zenobia shook her head back and forth. "Don't seem like to me your good-luck buckeye been workin too hard for you."

We held hands and slipped and stumbled acrost the rocks and branches in the crick and worked our way downstream in the shallows. The night closed around us. I could smell the wet earth, wild mint, and skunk. We sloshed through the water till we couldn't take another step, and finally, in the shelter of an overhangin sycamore, we dropped our packs and fell to the ground.

We was both shakin from the cold and the wet, gaspin like a couple of fresh-caught fish tossed on shore. Neither of us had the breath to talk.

Finally, Zenobia said, "Trapped in the cave weren't so good and safe."

I rolled onto my back. "Like I said, trapped ain't never good for the one in it." I looked up through the lacework branches of the trees, saw my first star, squeezed my eyes together, and made a wish for a table full of hot food.

We laid there, quiet, and all around us the night come into its fullness. Frogs, tree crickets, first one, then others, jar flies, all manner of sounds chorused together. Skeeters whined in my ears; I swatted, but no amount of hittin could keep them from feastin on me.

Above us, a lightnin bug circled and flashed. When I raised my head, I could see them flickerin on and off, like little candles in the bushes and grass alongside the crick.

"Zenobia," I said. "Look at them lightnin bugs. How can there be so much good and pretty and such bad and ugly all mixed together?"

I raked my fingers acrost the top of the grass and caught myself a handful of lightnin bugs, then sprinkled them over Zenobia's head. They snaggled into her dark, wiry hair, sparklin and flashin so's she looked like she'd walked into a cloud of stars.

Zenobia struggled up onto her elbows and looked down the crick. "I seen bad and ugly," she said, "but now I follers the North Star and finds me some good."

She laid back, tugged her food sack close, and clutched it to her body.

I pulled off my wet sling and spread it on the ground next to the sack, then I untied the knot, stuck my hand inside, and fumbled through apples. Finally, I felt at the softness of my old Hannah doll's skirt. Just rubbin on it made me feel safer.

Zenobia set up, reached into her bag, and pulled out somethin to eat. "We gots to get movin and find a place to hide out afore tomorrow mornin."

We rested, then gathered our sacks and hung them over our shoulders. I picked them lightnin bugs out of her hair and scattered them acrost the grass. Then, we stepped back into the cold crick and tossed water onto the bank to wash away our smell.

Every time I heard a hooty owl call or a dog fox bark,

I jumped. I were right used to bein outside, but tonight, I just wanted to settle down in front of a fire and sleep.

Zenobia and me walked for a few hours. We didn't talk none; it seemed like the water washed away all the words from us and sent them downstream. Finally, we heard the dawn song of a sparrow. *Old Sam Peabody, Peabody, Peabody,* it called, safe on its perch in a nearby tree. But there weren't no safe for us in the full light of day, and I were plumb out of ideas to keep us goin.

*If you're kind to the trees,
they'll tell your story ahead of you to the other trees,
and they will always lend you shelter.*

Zenobia and me was tired. I knowed we couldn't keep on walkin. I looked up into the branches of the huge sycamore where the little bird sang its song over and over, over and over. I wished I could feel so happy at the comin of the mornin.

Ten feet above us, a thick branch swooped acrost the crick, then dipped down almost into the water. I waded to the sturdy limb and pulled myself up and over, then dangled my legs on each side like I were ridin one of Grandpa's old horses. First I slid an inch, then another, and finally I hitched a few inches at a time till I got to the middle of the crick. Zenobia stood below me and watched as I hoisted myself up through the big branches, then up again till I were a good twenty feet above her. I looked down, through the wide leaf hands and branches, at glimpses of the curlin blue-green of the water.

"Get up here, trouble girl. You got no business bein down in the crick this time of day. Foller where I come up. There ain't no way for someone to track us up here from the middle of the water."

Zenobia checked her sack, tied it closed, and looked up into the thickness of leaves. She hugged the limb, pulled herself onto it, and crept to the center of the crick.

"I don't like this. I never like bein up high. What if I falls?"

"Turn your mind to climbin up and don't think nothin about fallin down," I urged.

Zenobia stood, steadied herself, and grabbed the branch above her. I watched her get her balance and walk slow toward the trunk. Once she reached it, she leant against its bulk, then gripped the branch and pulled herself up. At first, she were careful, but then she climbed faster and faster. Just as I started to caution her, she reached for a branch, and it snapped. She slipped, down, down, one limb, two, three, reachin, graspin, and hollerin as she fell toward the rocky crick below us.

"Hold on, girl!" I screamed.

She flailed, thumped, and stopped her fall in the fork of two strong limbs. They looked like big speckled arms cradlin her in the air.

"Oh law," I said. "Cain't you take care and get up here without near killin yerself and lettin everyone know we here?"

She looked up and shouted, "I didn't spect to be climbin no trees, and I sure didn't spect to be flyin through no trees."

"That weren't no flyin," I said, "that were fallin, and fallin and hollerin, and that ain't what we needs now."

Within a few minutes, she righted herself and began the climb through the branches, but she come more slow this time, not so bold and full of herself. Finally, she set on a limb just a few feet away. She were breathin hard and holdin on tight. Bloody scratches striped her arms, legs, and the side of her face. She looked like she'd been wrestlin a bobcat.

I could tell she hadn't spent no time in trees, but for me, hidin out high in tree branches always felt like a safe nest. Folks never think to look up. How many times had I run and hid from Pa and my brothers after they hurt me? They'd hunt through the woods never knowin that I set up above them and watched their every move.

When I pulled in my legs and arms and stretched full out along the thickness of the limb, no one would ever be able to see me. I reached out and patted the patchy trunk.

"We safe now, Zenobia. Just move closer to the trunk and keep your legs straight out so they don't show." I motioned her forward till she set close beside me. She slipped the torn pack off her back, looped the strap around her waist, and tied herself against the tree.

Zenobia shook her head. "I seen me some bears in trees, some birds, some possums, some squirrels, but never no slave girls." We giggled.

I reached out, pulled a danglin buttonball off a stem, and tossed it at her. She grabbed another, and afore we knowed it, we both had them buttonballs stickin to our clothes and hair.

"We best get restin and quietin down," I said. "We should be in Waterford town by tomorrow night."

"Why we goin close to a town?" she asked. "Town mean people. People gonna know we in trouble. Know we runaways."

"I been thinkin on it for a while, and Waterford's not like other towns," I said. "The preacher's wife told me them Quakers are good, kind folk, and right now I cain't think about anythin except tryin to find me some good, kind folk—and tryin to get some sleep." I snuggled against the tree; the branch swayed slightly and pieces of sunlight flashed through the big, papery leaves above us.

The faraway sound of a rooster's crow and the *chuck, chuck, chuck* of wood bein chopped carried acrost a wide meadow and rollin hills. Them was comfort sounds, like the sizzle of bacon or the purrin of a kitten. I reached into my sack, pulled out my patchwork Hannah, and tucked her under a strap. Then I patted at my pocket to make sure my lucky buckeye were still safe. Zenobia leaned back against the sycamore's broad trunk and closed her eyes.

"I wonder where my baby sister and my ma and papa be?" Zenobia asked. "I wonder if Promise still callin for me? Now our family all in pieces like your rag doll."

Family, I thought. I didn't know nothin about family, and now that my grandpa were gone, I wouldn't know what to do if any of my kin ever said a kind word to me. Hannah doll and Grandpa was the closest to family I'd ever had.

꒰꒱

I slept until the growlin and gnawin of my stomach woke me. I opened my eyes and stretched out slow and catlike.

Somewhere close by, I heard the voices of children, a man, and a woman yellin. I looked down through the leaves at what bits I could see of the ground below us. A big woman, dressed in men's clothes and high leather boots, stepped into the flickerin shade of the tree and glanced around. She bent over the earth, as though lookin for footprints, and called out to the others to hurry up.

Her deep, boomin voice woke Zenobia. She stretched, groaned, and shifted on the limb, not knowin that anyone were nearby. The branch swayed, and some of them sycamore buttonballs dropped down through the leaves and onto the woman-man below us.

*A mouth closed at the right time
is often wiser than an open one.*

I drew in my arms and legs and signaled Zenobia to do the same. When I peeped over the edge of the limb, I could see the woman-man knockin buttonballs out of her hair and off her shoulder. I pressed myself flat against the limb as she walked acrost the leafy ground below us.

Nearby, a flock of chatterin goldfinches dangled from the ripenin buttonballs and tugged at them. They called to each other, warbled their *see-me, see-me, chickoree,* and flew from branch to branch.

"Gold birds," the woman-man said in her gruff voice to nobody.

I opened my eyes wide and looked over at Zenobia. We

set, afeared to move, afeared to breathe, afeared to gaze down at the woman-man again, scairt she'd feel our stares.

My body ached from stayin put so long, and I knowed Zenobia were feelin it too. She stretched, stuck out her leg, and wiggled her toes back and forth. The branch didn't move, but I shook my head and wanted to scream at her not to chance it again.

"Over here!" the woman-man yelled. "We'll take cover here tonight."

Then clankin, a horse whinnyin, and voices below us.

Zenobia peered down through the branches and glanced at me, her eyebrows all knit together.

"What?" she mouthed, but I shook my head and held a finger in front of my lips.

I stuck my head over the edge of the limb and watched the happenins down below. Five tattered boys, three whites and two Negras, trickled into the clearin under the tree. One Negra, black as gunpowder and tall and straight as a young pine, were hog-tied to the other. A thin, weasel-faced man on a chestnut horse stopped beside the syca-more, swung out of his saddle, and tied the reins to a bush.

"I don't want to git no closer to a town or a road," the woman-man said. "We don't need no one snoopin our business, and we got water right here."

The weasel-face nodded and brushed dirt from his pants. "We'll keep 'em hid here tonight," he said.

Oh law, if they was thinkin to camp here all night, how could Zenobia and me stay in the tree?

Below us, one of the Negra boys began to sing a sad, sad song.

> "I'm troubled, I'm troubled, I'm troubled in mind,
> If Jesus don't help me, I surely will die.
> O Jesus my Saviour, on thee I'll depend,
> When troubles are near me, you'll be my
>   true friend."

"Stop!" the woman-man ordered. "Shut yerselfs up and don't make no more noise."

The singin stopped. I could hear murmurin, and then some talkin between them.

"I said shut up!" the woman-man shouted.

I leant over and peeked down.

The woman-man pulled a crumpled hat from her waistband and cuffed the two boys and kicked at their legs, just the way my pa always did me and the dogs.

The weasel-face tugged another piece of rope from his belt, looped it round the tree and the two hog-tied Negra boys, and knotted it.

"Y'all stay here," the woman-man ordered the boys. "Leave here and we'll find ya and whip ya till yer own mother wouldn't know ya."

I heard a low answerin, and then the woman-man and weasel-face untied their horses and led them toward the oak woods.

Three of them other boys set down under the tree and

talked quiet amongst themselves. The two black boys paced back and forth, back and forth on their short tethers, the way our hounds did when Pa tied them to the porch rails.

Them other boys wasn't chained nor tied, and I couldn't help wonderin why they didn't jus leave. Run for it. Hightail it to Waterford, or home, or wherever they wanted to go. But Pa hadn't never tied me—why had I stayed with him for so long?

The sun rode lower in the sky. Still the weasel-face and woman-man didn't come back. The two black boys stopped pacin and set down, their backs against the trunk like they needed to be propped up.

Zenobia wiggled and shifted again. This time the tree branches swayed. I reached over to rap on Zenobia's leg, and my Hannah doll slipped from under the strap and slid from my lap. I almost caught the hem of her patchwork skirt, but she were off and already on her way down through the limbs. She stopped fallin for just a moment as she caught on a big clump of mistletoe. "Thank ya, baby Jesus," I said to myself, but then Hannah, devil-bent to cause us trouble, come loose and disappeared through the leaves.

The boys stopped talkin. I imagined them lookin up, tryin to see where that doll come from.

It didn't take but a blink afore they was up and yellin at us.

"Git down here!" they called. "Git down here or we comin up to git ya."

"Thanks, trouble girl," I whispered. "You done it now. Got any ideas how to get us out of this?"

I couldn't help myself. I quick-like looked over the broad limb again and saw them, hands shadin over their eyes, lookin up into the tree. I ducked back down.

"You. You, girl!" one of the boys yelled.

He'd said "girl," not girls. He didn't know that there was two of us up in the tree. One of us were goin to be okay, but which one? And how could one of us be okay if the other got caught?

"Who does he see?" I asked Zenobia. "We cain't let them know they's two of us."

My question got answered afore we could decide what to do.

"Red," he yelled, "this is your last chance or we comin up after ya."

I looked over at Zenobia, mouthed a silent fare-thee-well, and began the long climb down.

Beware of those with eyebrows that meet;
in their hearts lies naught but deceit.

It seemed like a world of time afore I got to the ground and looked into the chicory-blue eyes of the boy who yelled. I thrust out my chin so I seemed growed up and like they didn't scare me none.

"What you want with me?"

The boy didn't say a word, just stared and stepped aside so's the shorter, white-haired boy, who were holdin my Hannah doll by a leg, could get up close. He looked from my head to my toes. I knowed that I were dirty and all tore up from washin down the crick, but I acted like I had on my clean Sunday clothes. Besides, he didn't look no better than me.

"You done now," the boy said. "You one of us, and you'll be workin for them too."

"Them? Why'd I be workin for them?" I looked from one boy to the other. "I works for myself now and nobody else."

"We all slaves, and nothin more. We're orphans. We might as well be black as them," the chicory-eyed boy said, noddin his head toward the bound-together Negra boys.

"Why don't you leave here?" I asked. "Leave here afore them people come back. You're not tied to nothin, and you sure can run and hide away from them."

"Been so long since we ate good, been so long we been travelin, I don't know where we run or what we'd do," the white-haired boy said to me. "Might as well be tied; if we run and they catch us, why, we'd be whipped to pieces."

I could feel all the others starin at me and listenin to our words. I looked round. They was all dirty and wore tattered clothes, and was barefoot except for the white-haired boy, who had on boots holier than my worm-eaten tobacca patch. I knowed I couldn't trust him, him with his two thick white eyebrows joinin together like one.

The Negra boys stood up and brushed dirt off their hands and pants.

"Easy you to hide," the tallest boy, with the scarred face and missin front tooth, said. "But I cain't. I'm a runaway, and they's takin me back to my owner. I tried runnin a few days ago and this is what it got me." He turned full round, and I could see his clothes all tore in slits and glued to his back with thick patches of dried blood.

"I know about that kind of hurtin. Pa and my brothers near broke me a few times," I said. "I run away afore, but they always caught me. Not now, though. I lit out of that place for good, and I aim to find me a new life."

"I don't know how you spect that," the white-haired boy said. "Nobody cares none what happens to us or to you. None of us got no family. We was sold to them, and now they're sellin us for bondslaves. Nobody cares."

"I care," I said. "I care what happens to you *and* what happens to me." I looked around the circle and saw some noddin their heads yes, others shakin them no.

"If'n we tell them bout you," the white-haired boy said, "they'll git us more food, take better care of us."

"No they won't," the scarred boy said. "They pack her in with us, and we won't get not a bite more, maybe even a bite less with another mouth to feed." He looked at me, gave me a quick half smile, then faced the others.

"You, you, boy, you stop talkin at us," the white-haired boy said as he shook his fist. "Who you think you are?" He dropped my Hannah doll and stepped right on her as he shoved the boy hard, then punched him in the stomach.

The boy buckled, straightened back up, and set his lips in a thin line. The other boy moved as if to step in, but the ropes held him tight.

I didn't see where this talkin and fightin were leadin me

to no place good. I started to say somethin to them about us all helpin each other when I heard people talkin and horse's *clop-clop*pin slow and easy toward us.

"Shhhh," I cautioned, my finger in front of my mouth. "Don't tell them nothin bout me."

I looked up at the sycamore—the first branch were just out of my reach. My Hannah doll laid on the ground by the black boy. I wanted to grab her, but I didn't have no time.

I run to the tree and jumped for the lowest branch, but missed it by an arm's length. The tallest Negra boy, the one with the scarred face, swung me up onto his broad shoulders and said, "Git out of here." I stood, reached up, grabbed the patchy limb, and pulled myself onto it.

I looked down, searchin for my Hannah doll, and saw the tall black boy bend over, pick her up, and stuff her inside his tattered shirt.

A horse whinnied.

I swished up and into the cover of the broad, leafy branches and climbed faster than I'd ever climbed afore. I looked for Zenobia, but for once she stayed put. Soon as I heard the woman-man and weasel-face gettin closer, I stopped, laid out flat on a limb, and hugged myself tight.

A fuzzy black-and-yellow-striped bumblebee hummed above me, circled, and landed on my arm. I didn't move. I watched as it stretched out its long tongue and licked itself like a cat, then combed its front legs down its dusty, furred body. It stopped, looked at me with its huge eyes, then packed its cargo of yellow dust into pockets on its rear legs. Its wings begun to move, and I could feel a tiny whirlwind in the hairs on my arms.

Below me another whirlwind exploded. Dogs barked and howled. Men shouted and cursed. I heard my pa's voice and the sound of the hounds. I felt like I were havin a nightmare with all the yellin and thrashin goin on. Old Delia dog were down there, snortin around the tree trunk, snufflin into the sand and leaves, raisin Cain.

"Where's the redhead girl? And where's my runaway slave girl?" Pa yelled. "I seen their tracks back a ways. Ya be hidin them and tryin to get the money, and I'll beat y'all till there ain't nothin left of your sorry hides. My hounds got the smell of them."

The woman-man yelled back at Pa, "Don't you be bustin in here, old man. Them're our boys, but them Negras over there, they're goin back to their owners. We caught them in Pennsylvania a week ago."

"Get outta here!" the white-haired boy yelled at the dogs, and he must've kicked at one by the sound of the yelpin.

I didn't have to see Pa to know he were mad.

He yelled to my brothers to look around the camp. I could hear them walkin through the leaves and shoutin to the dogs to stop their barkin.

"I don't know nothin about yer redhead girl," the woman-man yelled, "but you get out of here or we gonna shoot you like we shot the last man got in our way."

I heard rifles cock, then the sound of Pa mutterin.

Delia barked again, a high, yappin chirp like the one she gives when I tease her with a bite of food, then a short, yippin howl, the sound she makes when Pa kicks her.

"Movin out," Pa yelled to my brothers and the hounds. "That girl ain't nowhere round here, let's move it out."

They passed below me, so close I felt a chill run clear through my bones. I kept my eyes scrunched closed like I did when I hid inside the old pine chimney cupboard. If I couldn't see them, then they wouldn't see me.

Delia yipped and chirped again. I pictured her liftin her head, sniffin at the air between me and them.

My brothers yelled at Delia and Bathsheba; the woman-man and weasel-face shouted at them all to keep a-movin. I held my breath, not wantin them to smell my fear or feel my life above them.

They scuffled through the leaves below me, and Pa said, "Them dogs are tellin me them girls are round here somewheres. We're not goin far." They moved off, the dogs runnin in circles and barkin and Pa cursin a streak.

I laid still—still as that woman the preacher said turned into a pillar of salt. How long would it be afore one of them boys told the woman-man about me?

"What's this you hidin in your shirt?" I heard the woman-man ask. "Where the devil did this raggedy thing come from? Answer me," she shouted, *"now!"*

If an owl calls out a name,
that person soon will die.

I heard scufflin below me, but I didn't dare look down. Then, a muffled cry, and the scarred boy said, "I don't know where it come from. It were over by them tulip trees. When we was walkin over to here, I jus picked it up."

"Yer lyin," the woman-man shouted. "You saw them girls, and they's a reward for one of them. Which way did they go?"

No answer. I could hear someone whippin him, then yellin, and then some quiet, but still no answer. Were he goin to tell on me to save hisself from more beatin?

Even if he told, Zenobia would still be safe up here. No-body knowed about her.

My heart thudded, and I couldn't catch my breath. I wanted to open my eyes and look up to Zenobia again, just to feel like someone were with me, but I stayed still. Closed inside myself.

Mama, I thought, what is goin to happen to your girl now?

The man spoke up. "Let im be," he said. "We need to get im back fit to work or we won't get no reward."

The woman-man said, "This place been nothin but trouble for us. I come here thinkin it to be a good spot, all hid out under this big tree, water for the takin, but I'm not feelin safe."

A warm breeze lifted my hair like thin fingers was rufflin through it. Goose bumps stood up on my arms. Mama, I thought, is that your sperrit tellin me to hold on?

I held on but shook like a cottonwood leaf in a wind. Dust rose from all the commotion below me. I heard feet scufflin through leaves, talkin, and then the *clop, clop, clop* of the old horses movin slowly away.

Were Pa and my brothers somewhere nearby watchin for us? Me and Zenobia waited and waited, never passin a word to one another. Dark settled. I looked at Zenobia's wide eyes, then up through the tree at the comfort of the moon. It looked like it were snared in the branches.

"Zenobia," I whispered, "think we safe now? C'mon."

"Oh Lordy," she whispered. "Not bad enough climbin up, but now I gots to climb down, and in the dark."

"Stop your frettin and let your feet and hands find their way."

"Got your sling of food and bundle, my sack of food, and my tired body to move. I hope I don't do no flyin like last time."

"Just pay attention and talk to the tree. Thank it for givin us shelter."

"Thank ya, old tree," Zenobia sang quietly. "Thank ya for leaves and shade, and—" *Crack.* I heard the sound of wood splittin. Leaves and twigs showered onto me.

"Oh, Lark, I'm scairt to the bone. I cain't move."

"Come on, trouble girl. You sure don't have no choice but to come down or go up, and I cain't see how goin up will help you much. We got dark now, and we gots to move on while it's safe. Now, stay quiet."

I stood on the broad limb and reached up and patted Zenobia's bare foot.

"You're doin fine. Keep comin slow and easy-like, slow and easy, no hollerin and no flyin."

"You take your sack," she whispered as she swung it down to my branch.

I slid the sack onto my back next to my sling, thrust my leg into the black between the limbs, and felt for safe footin. I touched onto the smooth branch below me so's the steppin down come easy. First one foot, then another.

"It's not bad, Zenobia." Could she hear the shakin in my voice?

She sniffled above me.

"I wants to find my ma and papa, hold my baby sister again. I misses them till my heart burstin. But all I'm goin to do is end up broke into pieces or fish food in the crick."

"Quit feelin sorry for yerself." Although I were feelin right sorry for my own self. "We need to get away from here and find somewhere safe to hide for tomorrow, so climb down."

"I'm hungry," she whined.

"I'm hungry too, but we not safe around here. No tellin if Pa is close, if the dogs catches our smells again, or what—"

Crack. Zenobia flew past me, nearly knockin me off the limb. Fallin, fallin, down, down, just like my Hannah doll, without a sound. I heard her hit the ground with a loud thump, and then nothin.

My foot slipped. I caught myself, my heart poundin till it near jumped out of me. Were Zenobia hurt? Dead?

I felt my way slowly, brushin the limb with my feet, steppin down till I dropped from the last branch onto the sandy, leaf-covered soil. Zenobia and her sack laid like a heap of rags at the base of the tree.

"Zenobia? Trouble girl, answer me. Sorry, so sorry. You was so scairt, I should've helped you more." I bent over her and wiped the leaves and dirt from her face. Her arm were twisted behind her. Her eyes shut.

"Zenobia? Answer me, girl. You was so brave. Fallin like that and not a sound from you." A wind rustled through the sycamore leaves, and shiftin moon shadows washed acrost her bloodied face.

I laid my ear against her chest and tried to hear her heartbeat through the thickness of the night sounds. I shivered. Were somethin or someone watchin us? Then came a long dry shriekin cry, as cuttin and cold as a splinter of ice. I hunched over Zenobia's still body to protect her and looked all around us, up and down. Nothin stirred except the leaves.

Another shriekin. A pale barn owl, its heart-shaped face lookin down on us, flew by on silent wings and landed in the branches above.

"Night sperrit, don't you be callin out her name!" I shouted, shakin my fist up toward him. "I knows what happens when you calls a name."

"Zenobia. Trouble girl." I whispered so's the owl couldn't hear me. "We just found each other. We was like sisters. Now look what you gone and done."

*Death is foretold by a sound in the heavens
like a pack of animals at bay.*

I don't know how long I set there with Zenobia, rockin back and forth on my knees and cryin like I hadn't cried since my grandpa passed on. Oh, I knowed she were gone and that I'd have to bury her afore the day come on. I couldn't just walk away and leave her for the buzzards and animals. She needed a fittin restin place for her long journey home. My heart, my whole body hurt with a heavy load of sorrow.

I patted Zenobia, then pushed myself up. My legs and feet moved like they was wrapped in sacks. I stumbled toward the crickside, bent, and poked my fingers into the damp soil. It were loose and sandy, easy enough to dig, but I would need a sturdy branch and a flat rock to help with the work. Every sycamore stick I tried for diggin broke—too brittle for the task. I slid down the bank to the crick, turned over rocks, tossed some up the cliff to pile on Zenobia's grave, and chose a thin, flat stone for the diggin.

I slung our food sacks over the top of a bush, tied them together, and set off for the woods. I skirted the meadow so's to stay out of the fullness of the moonlight, and searched the ground for a strong stick.

The stick found me afore I found it. I stumbled, stepped down, and it reared up in front of me. I caught it, turned round, and headed back. I didn't want no animals to get to Zenobia afore I could take care of her.

Lightnin bugs flickered in the meadow. I thought on how Zenobia looked just last night with that cloud of them little stars shinin from her thick hair.

Were the moonlight playin tricks on me? Somethin flitted, moved through the grasses and wildflowers and in and out of the shadows, stopped, then vanished like a will-o'-the-wisp. I knowed if it were Zenobia's sperrit, I shouldn't be afeared, but my hands shook as I gripped the stick even tighter and melted into the bosky darkness.

Heels down first. Heels down slow and easy. I crept along, kept my eyes on a faint trail that spooled through the trees and tried to think like a deer. If I follered this, would I circle round and end up along the crickside near my friend?

Somethin snapped and crashed. Loud bayin and shriekin come at me from up above, beside me, all around. I stopped, my toes rooted into the ground. The frogs, the crickets, everythin quieted except the distant sounds of water. The night went quiet as an apple on a tree.

Maybe a minute passed, maybe more, but I didn't move. I learnt a long time ago that turnin into a shadow, disappearin into whatever was round me were sometimes the only way to stay alive. I knowed how to wait.

From somewhere close by come a familiar call. *Whip-poorwill, whippoorwill, whippoorwill.* The animals began singin their night songs again. I took one step, two, three, and slipped into the tangle of their sounds.

Soon I smelt the sycamores, heard the rushin of the crick, and knowed I were close to Zenobia.

Zenobia. My tongue licked at salty tears.

I'd need to get her in her grave, mound rocks on it so's no animal could reach her, and make my way toward Waterford afore the sun come up. I didn't have no plans, but I knowed that I wouldn't go back to Pa's house and the life, if I could even think on it as a life, I'd had afore trouble girl stirred things up for me.

The top of the big sycamore stood high above the other trees. I headed toward it, makin sure I stayed hid in the cover of the shadows.

I walked along the edge of the meadow, then stepped into the bright, freckled moonlight under the sycamore. On the limb above Zenobia's body set that white-faced owl. And on the bush where I'd tied our sacks of food were nothin.

*Slave children must always be buried
facedown to be set free to heaven.*

The stick felt like safe to me. I held it tight, rested it on my shoulder, and turned in a slow circle, searchin the shadows, the meadow, anywhere someone could hide. Silver-rimmed clouds run acrost the sky and smothered the moon. The dark under the tree turned blacker than a crow, too thick for me to see. The clouds passed. Slowly, slowly, things come into my sight, and I could see the empty bush.

My eyes darted back and forth, between Zenobia and the woods. I shook and my skin turned cold, like it done when Pa put his eyes on me. More bad would happen.

Were it Pa out there watchin and just waitin to catch

me and drag me back to his cabin? Worst of all, takin me away and leavin Zenobia alone, unburied, critters tearin and worryin at her like she'd never been nothin to no one. But she had been. She had a family that loved her, and she were my onliest true friend—the first one since my grandpa who cared what my brothers and Pa done to me. She were the one who fitted me with my name. She would be buried proper by me—and not facin down like a slave. Zenobia were a free girl when she died.

I stooped beside Zenobia, wiped my tears with the gritty back of my arm, and whisper-sang, "Back in the lovin arms of Jesus, precious Jesus take me home" to make myself feel easy. I moved alongside her, takin care not to step over her body so's I wouldn't end up in the grave with her.

I walked over to the bank and stretched out on the ground where I were goin to dig the buryin hole, scuffed my feet, and dragged my hands against the sandy soil for a size marker. If someone watched me, they must be thinkin that I been bit by a crazy dog.

My stomach knotted and growled so loud it sounded like it come from an animal. Hungry, tired, thirstin, and runnin out of night. No time to stop and eat. Some mess of trouble if the job weren't done soon.

I knelt beside the crick and filled my cupped hands with water again and again till my stomach swolled and wouldn't hold another sip. I still hungered. Inside my pocket was the leathery dried wintergreen leaves. I tore off a little wad of them and chawed. That first shock of mint made my mouth water. Then I chawed and chawed on them leaves to ease my hunger.

I dipped my hand into the water, felt along the bottom of the crick like a raccoon lookin for crawdads, and lifted out two small, smooth stones for settin Zenobia's eyes.

I couldn't put off what had to be done a minute longer. I crawled up the bank, found my markers, picked up my stick, and began breakin through the ground. *Thump, thump, thump.*

The flat rock worked like a hoe, cuttin through the soil and moundin it so's I could scoop it with my bare hands onto the ground beside me. Sweat ran burnin into my eyes. My self got lost in the rhythm of the poundin, the scrapin of the stone, and the swoosh of the earth as I tossed it aside. Slowly, slowly, minute by minute, the hole got bigger and deeper.

I stopped, leant on the stick, and looked up at the night sky. The thick whiteness of the Milk-Away spilt acrost the wide blackness. I searched out the Drinkin Gourd, and found the four bowl stars and the three in the handle pointin to the steadiness of the North Star—the star Zenobia once follered to find her free soil.

"Mama, Grandpa, what a fine place to be. Down in a grave hole, and fair game for anyone huntin me. And now my friend will be buried here forever." I brushed at a tear.

The grave weren't near as deep as the one Grandpa'd been put in, but I'd dug down so's I stood waist deep. I dropped my stick and pushed myself up with my wobbledy arms, but the wall of the grave crumbled. Sand, small stones, rocks, and clumps of soil slipped right back where they'd just come from. Dirt covered my feet. I set back for a minute's rest and leant against the side of the grave. The moon disappeared behind the trees, and darkness poured into the hole. Smells of damp earth, wet leaves, and skunk wrapped around me. A toad purred, and the owl, the owl, it shrieked once, took wing, and glided, like a death haint above me.

Somethin slithered acrost my foot, and I clawed my way out of the grave hole and onto the ground. I lay there on my back, pantin, and closed my eyes. The sycamore leaves rustled loudly, and my skin prickled till the hairs on my head felt like they was stickin straight out. My eyes flew open and there, starin down from the tree, were a dark, shadowy ghost face with big, dark eyes.

*You can bewitch someone by pointing
any sharp stick or cane at him.*

Could the face have been a shape-shiftin trick of the shadows? I propped up on one arm, craned my neck so's to see into the branches, but it, whatever it were, had vanished.

I were scairt—scairt so deep inside—but I needed to stay, needed to finish what I started.

The stars faded, and the first gray light of dawn sifted through the leaves and onto Zenobia. She needed buryin, and soon. My achin body wanted to stay restin, but my head told me it were time to get up and take care of my friend.

I reached into my pocket and felt for my lucky buckeye.

"I should've give this to you, Zenobia," I said to nobody. "Don't know how I'm goin to do this to you, girl. Bury you here, for forever." Tears trickled down my face. There weren't no shirkin this job. She needed to be brushed clean and set to rights like I did my grandpa in his pine box. She'd be laid out, hands folded over her chest. Then, the flat stones set onto her eyes, and a bunch of wildflowers tucked into her hands to keep her company. I dropped to my knees, straightened her raggedy skirt and her bent leg careful, so as not to hurt her. But how could I hurt her any more than she were? I reached under her body to straighten her arm and tugged it.

"Aiiieeeee! Aiiieeeeeeeeeee!"

I dropped Zenobia's arm and tripped backward over a root just as somethin heavy—heavy and big—tumbled from the tree and landed half on me. When I fell against Zenobia's body, my screamin tailed onto the other screamin sound. Sure as thunder after lightnin, I knowed the haints was goin to put me in that grave with her.

❧

I laid there twined in a jumble of black and brown arms and legs—like snakes in a rock pile. "Lark, you be killin me," a familiar voice cried.

"How can I be killin you if you dead?" I asked, lookin down into Zenobia's wide golden eyes.

One long black leg worked its way out of the tangle, and

a big hand pushed against me. I looked back and watched the gunpowder-black slave with the scarred face strugglin to stand. Last time I seen him he were hog-tied onto another boy.

I raised up, felt at myself to make sure all the pieces was still there, and started to move off Zenobia, and she cried out again.

"I'm hurtin, hurtin bad," she said.

"You be hurtin with no skin on your back if you don't keep quiet," the runaway boy said. "You scairt me right off that branch when you come back from the dead."

"She's hurt bad," I said. "We need to help her."

"I know what happen to me when I try to help someone besides my own self," the boy said. "Look what helpin you done for me."

I looked at his bloodied legs and arms, and my stomach turned.

"Sorry," I said, my head bent. When I looked up, I could see my Hannah doll's head pokin out of his shirt.

This weren't no time for us to talk about what had happened to him or how he'd gotten away from them slave catchers. We needed to get away afore the sun come up over the hills.

"I gotta move you, trouble girl," I said, "but you cain't make a sound. I'll be as easy as I can, but if you scream again, after all that noise we made, well, our luck is about played out."

Zenobia looked at me and nodded.

The boy stood behind me and dropped to his knees, his face all twisted with hate. He looked at me like he'd tasted spoilt meat. He jumped down into the grave hole and crawled back out with the long diggin stick tight in his fist. Were he so mad at me from the trouble I'd caused him?

I watched him get up and walk toward me, the stick pointin steady at me all the time. I knowed what he were doin and turned my head so as not to be caught in his witch trickery. I glanced back at him again, takin care not to look at the stick. He come closer. It took all of everythin I had inside me to turn my back on him. If he were goin to end my days, I wanted helpin Zenobia to be the last thing I done on earth.

*If you see a flock of birds, make a wish
and do not look back at the birds again
or your wish won't come true.*

Crack! I shrunk myself down over Zenobia to protect
her and couldn't help myself from lookin back over my
shoulder.

The boy stood behind me, that long stick split into two
pieces. He bent over Zenobia and said, "You got yerself a
broke arm. We'll set it on this stick, but it goin to hurt."

Zenobia rolled slow-like onto her good side and let out a
cry. I could see her arm all crumpled backward.

We set her up, propped her against the tree, and the
pain, the pain, it made her black out.

"Quick," the boy said. "Help me get her arm straight."

We worked fast, and though Zenobia's eyes was closed like she were fast asleep, she moaned and whimpered.

"Now lay that stick onto it," he ordered.

I set the stick against Zenobia's crooked arm and held it.

The boy jumped up and ran to a bundle on the ground that must have fell down from the tree with him.

"Our sacks!" I said.

He just looked at me, grabbed my torn apple sling, reached inside, and pulled out some jerky to gnaw.

When he passed me a piece of my own meat, I said a thank-you and then wondered why I were thankin someone for givin me somethin he stole from me.

The boy and I worked quick, windin and windin the strip of white cloth around the stick and the arm until both was wrapped like a cocoon.

Zenobia moaned again. I ran to the edge of the crick, dipped my skirt into water, and come back to wipe all the blood and dirt from her scratched, tear-streaked face.

"Lark, Lark," she whispered. "We gots to leave this hainted place. Lark, my arm on fire, on fire."

Zenobia slipped back, her eyes closed, her head lolled to one side.

"Girl," the boy said. "Help me lift her and lay her over my good shoulder."

I held Zenobia against the tree. The boy got onto his knees, stuck his head through Zenobia's good arm, and stood with her danglin over his shoulder, loose as a rag doll.

"Which way we goin?" he asked.

"East," I said.

"Why not north?" he asked. "North to free soil?"

"Toward the risin sun," I said, and pointed at the thin line of pink beginnin to color the sky. "We're goin to Waterford. Nobody will be expectin us to head east to a town."

"Towns ain't nothin but trouble—trouble and peoples," the boy said, shakin his head at me.

"This one is different," I said. "It's a Quaker town, and they'll help us find a safe way north. Leastwise as safe as we could ever be."

"You tellin me that everyone there is good, cause I don't believe it," he said. "I ain't met many good whites."

"My preacher's wife told me that most of them Quakers are good. We just have to watch and take our chances. It's our only hope," I said.

The big boy turned and walked into the woods carryin the weight of Zenobia like she were a bird bone. Quietly, almost so quietly that I couldn't tell if I were imaginin it or hearin it, the runaway said, "Look for signs." Not a twig snapped nor a leaf crackled as they disappeared into the forest.

What'd he mean by "look for signs"?

I hoisted our sacks onto my back and picked up a leafy hickory branch to brush our footprints from the sandy ground. *Swish, swish,* I worked my way backward, felt something soft under my toes, and looked down. Smilin up at me were my raggedy, dirty Hannah doll. I grabbed her up and brushed at her, then tucked her into my sack.

"Welcome back, Hannah," I said, grinnin like I'd just found myself a lucky ear of red corn. Maybe things was goin to get better for us now.

When I reached the meadow, I turned and threw the leafy branch over the bluff and into the bend of the rushin crick. No footsteps told the story of where we'd been, but I knowed that the dogs could still smell us. I prayed for a rain to come afore Pa and the dogs come back this way.

I run for the cover of the woods. The three lumpy sacks poundin against my back slowed me down some. Just as the sun rose above the tree line, I stepped into the welcome darkness of the forest. At first, I couldn't see nothin, but my eyes soon grew used to the dim light. I searched the ground for a sign that would tell me which way the runaway and Zenobia had gone, but there was no tracks. How could they disappear so fast when they only started runnin a few minutes afore me?

What if I couldn't find them? What if I never saw Zenobia again? Worst yet, what if they was caught?

Small patches of sunlight slanted through the branches. I follered a narrow trail toward the east and stopped by a sassafras tree to peel off a curl of bark for chewin. I picked one of the mitten-shaped leaves, held it up to my hand, then tucked it into my shirt for good luck.

I walked steady, and when I broke into the blindin

sunlight of a clearin, a deep sound like big guns boomed above me.

The sky turned dark with the wings of wood pigeons. I wanted to make a wish on them then turn away, but afore I had the chance, there were a loud *boom, boom, boom* that echoed through the trees. Pigeons fell from the sky.

Boom, boom, boom, the shots come again, but this time the pigeons kept circling as though they was all one.

Boom, a shot crashed into a nearby tree, and a huge chunk blew apart. Someone were shootin at somethin, or someone, or me. I took off runnin.

If a rabbit crosses your path,
follow him and make a circle
around him for good luck.

Thump, thump, thump. The sacks hit my back as I ran, jumpin over fallen logs and skirtin rocks.

I never slowed, never slowed for a second until the sounds of gunfire was far behind me.

I run deeper into the woods searchin for a hidin tree where I could sit and watch the trail without anyone seein me. A rabbit scuttled past and dived into an openin in the brush. I dropped to my knees, ducked my head, and crawled in behind it, twigs and vines snappin at my face and stickery burrs clingin to my hair. There weren't no chance of me circlin round him to catch me some good luck.

Ahead of me, a knob of mossy boulders, patchy with ferns, stood near a pool. A thin stream run down the biggest rock and dripped into the dark water. The rabbit stopped, slowly lapped at the water, then hopped away.

The sacks slid off my shoulders and dropped to the ground. I sank next to them and felt grateful for the cool and the quiet. Then I saw it. A small dipper gourd, twine tied through its handle, set beside the pool.

My fingers run acrost the inside of the gourd and felt water. Someone had just been here, drunk from this dipper, and left quick. I searched the ground for footprints, hopin it had been Zenobia and the runaway, but found nothin, nary a hint of who'd been here.

I drunk my fill, then rubbed myself with a handful of wild mint to keep the skeeters and flies from eatin at me. The scuppernong, climbin up and over the bushes and into the trees, hung with fat clusters of brown-green fruit. I picked and picked, stuffin them into my mouth—six, seven, ten at a time, just like the greedy jay at the top of the tree.

Zzzip. A mite of a hummingbird wearin a bright-red collar flew up and down the stalks of cardinal flowers just beginnin to open. I watched, losin myself in the doins of the tiny bird. He hovered near the ground and snapped up a midge, and then I saw it. A sign.

White pebbles was laid like an arrow, pointin toward a nearly invisible grassy trail leadin into the heart of the woods. Did the runaway boy leave it there for me to foller?

The arrow. Should I go the way it pointed or choose my own path?

"Mama, what should I do?" I asked.

My feet wanted me to go in another direction, but my heart—and I can't never be sure my heart is right—made me foller where the arrow pointed. I lifted up my sacks, tucked the gourd inside so's no one would guess anyone had been here, and walked toward the trail.

I looked back, checked to make sure I hadn't left anythin behind, then kicked the arrow apart and patted the sack to feel for my Hannah doll.

The wind stirred the trees, and I smelt the comin rains and heard the plashin on the leaves afore I felt the first drops. Then, all aslant from the east come a curtain of rain. Rain were good for my travelin—it kept folks indoors, and it washed away my scent. I hummed quietly, then sang to myself, "Rains from the east, three days of rain at least." I guessed I could stand the rain if it kept me safe. Safe or not, my wet clothes and wet hair made me shiver, though I felt burnin hot inside.

The rain fell harder. Nobody would hear me or see my footsteps today. The trail dipped into a holler and disappeared. What if someone, the someone who had left the gourd behind, were hidin, waitin down there for me? My body wanted to move, but it felt like my feet was spiked into the trail. I bent over, picked up a rock, and held tight to it as I walked to the edge of the holler and looked down.

Plonk. A pebble bounced off my back and rolled away. *Plonk,* another hit on my shoulder. I turned just in time to see a young red-haired boy, in torn brown pants and a bright-blue shirt, runnin away.

*July third to August eleventh are
the dog days and can be the most
unlucky days of the year.*

Should I keep goin east toward Waterford, where I told
the boy to run to? Should I turn and head north? I argued
inside myself, tryin to figure what my pa would expect
me to do and where the runaway and Zenobia would go.
East, west, north? No matter that I'd told him to head for
Waterford.

I took a step, then stepped back, shook my head, and
headed east again. I shivered and hugged tight to myself.
My mind wandered to the cabin, where my narrow bed set
beside the stove. How I would love to burrow underneath
Mama's warm quilt, but I had to keep on walkin.

I looked down. There, laid out in a line, were another long twig arrow pointin my way.

"Just walk," I ordered myself. "Foller them, one, two, three." Somehow countin each step kept me goin along the trail. I walked over the twigs, kicked them apart, and kept on.

What were the worst thing that could happen if Pa caught me? He'd give me a beatin, a bad beatin, and drag me back to the cabin. I were just as much a slave as Zenobia and the boy. But now that I had spent some days without the beatin and the shamin, well, if he caught me, I would just bide my time and run away again. Somehow I would break free. I knew, though, that for the runaway boy and Zenobia, things would be worse, much worse, if they was caught.

Ahead of me I could see a short, arrow-tipped run of shiny white pebbles. I headed toward them and scuffled through the line.

The sun stood straight above the trees, and the day turned mean and hot. I looked up at the clearin sky and down at my soaked clothes—they steamed like a boilin kettle. I shook, shook so much my teeth clacked together. I were burnin hot and freezin cold all at once. My head ached, ached so much I felt like cryin, but there weren't nothin for me to do cept try to keep walkin.

I wiped at my sweaty face and reached into my pocket to rub the smooth of my buckeye.

"Keep goin, girl," I said aloud. "Mama, am I goin the right way?" My eyes burnt till it hurt me to look at the trail.

"Ninety-nine, one hunnert," I said, still countin my steps.

"One hunnert and one," I said, thinkin on how my life changed for the good, even with all the bad, after Zenobia and I found each other. But now I had other problems, like worryin about Zenobia when I'd never worried about no one else afore. I missed her, missed havin the feel of a true friend and sister. Even with all the worryin bound up around her, it were still better to have her in my life than not.

"Two hunnert," I mumbled.

I walked steady on, stoppin only to pull stickers out of my bloodied feet and to try to keep from shiverin. Once in a while I would come upon another line of pebbles or another twig arrow and brush it apart with my foot as I passed. I kept on walkin, but my body felt like it'd been mule-kicked.

Had the black boy left the signs for me? Or did the rock-throwin red-haired boy leave them? Were I walkin to a safe place? Or walkin straight into a trap?

I don't know how I kept a-goin, but by late afternoon, the woods ahead of me thinned, and I could see sunny meadows and fields. Waterford town must be nearby. I slowed, slipped my sack down, pulled out some meat and a slice of apple, and stood chewin like our old cow, Hildie.

"Look for signs." Those words kept dancin round me, weavin in and out of my head and tauntin me.

My curiosity tickled and nudged, but I were so tired, so sick, that I could barely creep to the edge of the woods. I looked acrost at a town that seemed as tiny as the acorn villages I built under our big oak tree. Stone and brick houses, barns, stores, a mill, what looked to be a church, a blacksmith's shop, and a school dotted the land. On the outskirts set a small gray log cabin surrounded by a tall fence and a patchwork garden of flowers. Clothes flashed and swung on a line. A dog barked, and in the field, a man moved a scythe back and forth, back and forth, steady as the pendulum of my grandpa's old mantel clock.

No walkin acrost the open fields durin the daylight. I looked up and around at the trees, and picked a likely one to climb. I tied my sacks together and slung them over the lowest branch, then hoisted myself up, then up again, draggin the sacks behind me. I were some slow now, the cold shiverin all mixed up with the hot sweat comin through my skin and soakin my already-wet clothes. I climbed high enough so's I could see clear acrost the fields, then tied the sacks to a branch and settled in for the rest of the afternoon. I don't know how long I perched there, but I dozed on and off, sweatin and shakin, then wakin when the sounds of loud voices and barkin dogs seeped in and out of my dreams.

I pinched myself on the arm. "Mama, am I awake

or asleep?" I asked. My wakin world and sleepin world mixed together inside me.

More barkin and yellin. The wind blew from the east, lucky for me, carryin my scent away from the dogs. I ducked my head down, blinked my eyes to clear the blurriness, and peered through branches toward the town. From where I set, I could see groups of men runnin from house to house. The dogs run ahead of them, circled and lunged, howled and bayed. Them dogs went wild when they got to the fence surroundin the little gray log cabin.

I saw someone step out of the cabin and walk to the fence, then watched as other people streamed down a pathway and stopped outside the yard. I've got some keen hearin, but I couldn't tell what were goin on.

Then I saw him. The young boy in the bright-blue shirt run up to the men, talked to them, waved his arms, and pointed toward the woods.

"Oh law," I said. "Wind blowin west or not, I'm caught now. These are the dog days, and nothin good can come of them."

Everythin went quiet, or went quiet in my head, cause them dogs never did quit their barkin. I started to climb down and then stopped. What good would it do? Lord knew that I didn't have enough time or strength to get down and hightail it.

A shooting star is a sign that someone's soul is journeying to heaven.

The men and dogs left on a run. I couldn't understand what had just happened. The boy knew that I were somewhere west of town, but he sent them the other way. My breath caught and took, and I realized that I'd been holding it inside me while I watched. I clung tight to the tree.

The day spent, but I lost track of it, wakin and sleepin, burnin inside, and never knowin what were real or dreams. I knew I were some sick, and I didn't know how long I could hold on.

Night come. Soft light shone from windows, and shadows moved back and forth acrost them. The smell of woodsmoke and meat drifted over the field, makin me yearn for a cooked meal.

I reached into the fattest sack, pulled out another hard piece of dried meat, and chewed it slow. I were thirstin, thirstin so bad that all I could think of were water, sweet water fillin my mouth and tricklin down my burnin, sore throat.

Up through the tree branches, I saw a star streak acrost the sky. I hoped that didn't mean Zenobia or the runaway was bound for heaven.

Branch by branch I made my way down, the sacks draggin and catchin. Finally, I dropped them at the foot of the tree, then swung myself down beside them. I stuffed a handful of apple slices into my mouth, patted my Hannah doll, and shouldered the sacks.

My foot stepped on a small rock. I bent over, picked it up, wiped it on my skirt, and stuck it into my mouth. Rollin it around, suckin on it, just suckin at that rock set my mouth to waterin.

"Here we go, Mama," I whispered.

Pickin my way through the woods got harder. Every time I set down my foot I wondered if I could ever lift it again to take another step.

I broke past the last fringe of trees and walked the edge of a meadow. In front of me, another arrow of shiny white pebbles pointed to a knee-high field of corn. I kicked at the pebbles, sent them flyin, and kept walkin.

Lights in the town went out one by one. The moon shone acrost the fields and glinted on the corn like it were silver. I squatted, watched, and listened. I heard the rushin water of the millrace, the creakin of the mill wheel, and the rustlin of the corn. I could smell the sweet pine of the mill, and from somewhere nearby, a catbird called and mewed, but not a soul moved.

Another arrow-tipped line of shiny white pebbles pointed to a narrow pathway. I scuffed the pebbles aside and crept toward the outskirts of the sleepin town.

The lights from the window of the little gray cabin made three yellow patches. I headed toward them without payin attention to where I were—until I stubbed my toe and looked down. I were on the edge of a buryin ground, small gravestones pricklin through the grass like thumbs. A long stone buildin stood on a rise above me, its moon shadow markin an inky darkness.

I backed out. That weren't no place I wanted to be; bad, bad luck to walk into a buryin ground at night. I shivered again, this time from bein scairt and bein cold and hot all mixed together. I picked up a handful of dirt and sifted a thin line of it through my fingers and onto the ground between me and the graves. No haint would dare cross over and foller.

One of the lights went out in the cabin. Now it looked like two yellow eyes stared out at me.

Somethin thudded. I stopped in the middle of a step, my sacks thumpin against my back. I heard a sound like laundry bein shook out, and then a slap as somethin slammed.

When I looked down, I saw another line of shiny white pebbles runnin alongside a crickity, knobblety wooden fence. Tall hollyhocks peered over the top, and moths big as my hands flew in and out of their cup blooms. So still, so still and peaceful, that I could hear the whirrin of their wings.

I stopped and watched the little cabin. Nothin moved.

My hand skipped along the palins of the fence, one by one, till I reached the front gate. The smell of roses, mint, and sage wrapped round me.

When I looked down, I saw another short line of pebbles pointin toward a porch. I nudged them with my feet so's nobody would see them and walked through the gate. Below the porch, a large pot, stinkin with the smell of lye, bubbled and boiled. Beneath it, a bed of coals glowed a wicked orange. I looked toward the cabin and saw first one, then the other window darken.

I stepped through the gate and looked around the yard, then slowly walked up a camomile pathway. Every step smelt like apples.

"Thee is welcome here," a quiet voice said.

I turned and started to run, but my knees crumpled and my feet felt like two heavy stones.

The voice come again, soft, wavery, like water ripplin acrost a pond.

"Thee is welcome here, friend," the voice said again.

Welcome here? How could I trust anyone? My legs shook, and my eyes filled with tears. That was the last thing I remembered.

*Never hurt a spider
or you will suffer bad luck.*

A muzzy red light and a low roarin inside my head made me feel all pain and thirstin. I fought to pull myself away from Pa. He grabbed at me, held on to my foot, and yanked.

I kicked, yelled, and kicked again, fightin hard, but couldn't break away from his hands. Dogs howled and snarled around me. Weren't nowhere for me to go, no way for me to get freed.

A shard of sunlight pierced through the darkness inside me. When my eyes opened, I saw that my feet was caught, wound tight up in a bedsheet. I kicked free and set up. When I looked down at myself, I saw that my clothes was gone. I were in a clean white nightshirt sewed from cotton feed sacks.

The room weren't like any I'd ever seen. It were tiny and held only a tall, narrow bed, a small table with a white pottery pitcher and cup, a colorful braided rug, and a rockin chair with a woven splint seat. A big, chipped thunder bucket set on the floor beside the table. High above me near the peak of the roof, a long, narrow openin covered with wooden slats let in thin, bright stripes of sunlight.

At the foot of the bed, I could see the outline of a short, wide door. I wanted to crawl to it, try to see where I were, but I didn't have the strength.

Water, I needed water. I rolled onto my side, reached for the cup, and lifted my head till I could sip. I didn't want to stop drinkin, but the tiny room spun around me. I laid back on the pillow, the cup still in my hand.

"Where am I, Mama?" I asked. "Where am I?"

Sleep come easy to me. When I woke, the room were almost dark. A bowl of warm broth set next to the pitcher of water and the cup. I pushed myself up and leant against the wooden spindles of the bed.

It didn't take me no time at all to drink down all the water and start on the broth. I could taste bits of chicken, onions, and carrots. When were the last time I had eaten somethin cooked and hot?

I finished and swung my legs over the edge of the bed and stepped down onto the thick, braided rug. When I tried to stand, my legs was wobbledy, as wobbledy as our cow Hildie's newborn calf.

"Mama, can you hear me? Help me find some good luck."

I held on to the bed, slid myself down along the mattress, and reached for the door, shoved, shoved harder, but it wouldn't budge. My fingers worked along the edge of it in search of a crack, a pull, anythin that would help me open it.

Were I a prisoner? Would I be sold and sent away like Zenobia's family? I felt scairt and near at my wits' end, but kept tryin to open the door. By now it were dark in the room. Darker than night, dark like it had been in the cellar hole—I couldn't do no more.

The bed were only steps away, but I felt like I'd walked for miles. I slumped down onto the mattress. The last thing I remembered were the sweet smell of lavender.

When I woke, the sun shone through the high, slatted openin under the eaves. A fat brown spider dangled from a thin strand above me, then swung over to the edge of the chair. I licked at my cracked lips and tried to sit up. I watched the spider as she walked from the edge of the table to the rockin chair and back again, layin a silver strand of web behind her.

Grandpa's song about spiders played over and over in my head. "Let a spider run alive, all your days you'll live and thrive." That were all I wanted, to live and thrive.

The bowl of broth were gone; in its place set a thick slab

of bread. I reached for the water, drunk my fill, and for the first time in I don't know how long, ate a piece of bread smeared with butter and scuppernong jam. Nothin had ever tasted better.

I drifted off to sleep again, still hearing Grandpa's song. I jerked awake and set up. Had someone been singin to me? Touchin me with cool, soft hands?

A steamin bowl of barley porridge set on the table. The water pitcher, filled to the top, dripped and puddled beside the cup. Who were bringin food and drink to me?

I drank water, picked up a horn spoon, and ate the thick porridge. When I finished, I pushed myself up from the bed and walked acrost the little room. My fingers run along the edge of the door, and down near the bottom I felt a small iron pull. When I reached for it, my hand shook so much I could barely slide my fingers through the loop. I tugged, tugged again, and felt the door move slightly. My heart beat hard, and I breathed as fast as when I run through the woods.

What would I do when I got the door open? Where could I go? Where were my real clothes, my sack and food, my lucky buckeye, and where were my old Hannah doll?

I slipped down the wall and set beside the door. Finally, I said aloud words my grandpa used to say to me. "Don't be scairt, Sweet Girl, just get movin."

The door made a small creakin sound when I pulled on the loop. I held my breath, pulled again, and it budged the tiniest bit. What if someone heard me tryin to get out? I waited for a minute, put my ear against the door, and listened. No sounds. When I tugged again, the door moaned and opened a crack. I waited, then pulled harder. It opened an inch, then wider. I held the edge of the door with both my hands. One more jerk, and it opened full on to a solid brick wall.

*If you hear a crow calling, it is a sure sign
of death. Spit over your left and right shoulders
and call out to the crows to fly away and take death with them.*

I stood there starin at the wall like some kind of fool.
Then I reached out and patted at it. It were real. Real and
hard, and nary a crack nor sliver of light to show that there
had ever been anything there but a wall.

I stopped, laid my ear against the bricks, and listened.
Were someone movin acrost the floor on the other side?

I looked around the room for somethin, anythin to pick
at the brick, but the closest thing to a tool were the horn
spoon settin in the porridge bowl. I started for the spoon,
then stopped. "Girl," I said. "You could chip away at that
brick wall for a year of Sundays and not get yerself out
of here."

"Yessum," a deep voice whispered.

I swung round. The room were empty. My heart pounded.

"I must be goin out of my head," I said, doubtin that I'd heard a real voice.

"Yessum, you must be goin out of your head," the deep voice answered.

I shivered. Someone or somethin were in the room with me.

I turned in a slow circle, my eyes searchin everywhere but not wantin to find anythin.

"Am I dreamin again?" I asked.

No answer, just quiet.

I pinched myself hard on the arm.

"Ouch, I am not dreamin."

Quiet.

"Where are you?" I asked, mad and scairt all twisted together inside me.

Quiet.

I shuffled slowly acrost the room, looked beside the bed, under the bed, and in the corners, but found nothin.

"Am I a prisoner?" I asked.

Quiet.

I looked up, down, held my breath, and waited for an answer, but the only sounds was the nearby *caw, caw, caw*in death calls of crows and the wind whistlin through the wooden slats high above me.

I spit over both shoulders and asked the crows to fly

away and take death with them. Were that voice a death sperrit come lookin for me?

What were happenin? Were I a prisoner? Where were Zenobia? Were she caught and a prisoner now too?

The thick heat of summer had turned the little room into an oven, and I felt all played out. I climbed onto the bed and curled up like my grandpa's old Delia dog. I felt too scairt to close my eyes, but I must've closed them and dozed, because I woke to the sound of a dull clunk and somethin slidin and scrapin below me.

My heart thumped. I pushed myself up and looked around the darkenin room, but I were alone. My fist pressed against my mouth, as though I could hold all my courage inside.

Another clunk and one big dark hand appeared beside the bed, snaked up, twisted, and turned full round, almost like it had eyes and were searchin for me.

I pressed my fist harder against my lips, bit into it, and moved back against the wall to get as far from the hand as I could. It slipped down the side of the bed and disappeared.

The bed shook. Now two big hands come. They reached up and pulled at the edge of the mattress.

I heard a loud scream. The scream come from me.

When someone calls your name, don't answer
until you know who is talking or you may end up
doing the devil's bidding.

Them big hands let go and disappeared.

I rolled over, grabbed the thunder bucket from its place on the floor, and stood up on the saggin corn-husk mattress that crackled with my every move. Whatever, whoever were comin into the room would have a heavy stinkin surprise dropped on top of it.

A cool gust of air rushed in from somewhere below. My arms and legs turned rough as chicken skin, and my hair prickled. I looked around at empty.

"Lark," someone hissed, "Lark."

Were the trickster death sperrit callin me again?

"Lark, it's me."

I stood ready to drop the bucket.

"Lark, it's me, Zenobia," the voice whispered, but I didn't believe it.

"How do I know it's you and not the devil?" I asked.

"Who else call you Lark?"

The braided rug took on a life and slipped to the side of the table below me. I couldn't believe what I were seein. A trapdoor slid full open. More cool air come into the room. Two big dark hands rose up again, reached for the mattress, and pulled at the edge of the bed. I took aim.

Up come the scarred face of the tall boy who had carried Zenobia away from me.

He looked at me. "Lark," he said, "don't you be droppin that bucket on me."

He pulled hisself out of the trapdoor, rolled onto the floor, and set up.

He looked clean now and were dressed in real clothes, not the bloodstained filthy rags he'd worn the first time I seen him with the soul drivers.

I lowered the bucket and walked to the edge of the bed.

Seein his face peerin up at me, seein that he were a real boy and not a death sperrit made my stomach settle.

"There someone behind me that you be glad to see," he said.

The big boy reached down and tugged and up come Zenobia, one arm all wound in strips of fabric and tucked into a sling.

I leapt from the bed, set the bucket on the floor, and wrapped my arms gently around her.

"Quiet," he said. "We cain't make no noise."

Outside, the sound of thunder clapped and rattled the cup against the pitcher, and a steady, hard rain began to fall.

The boy slid the trapdoor closed and pulled the rocker close to us. Zenobia and me set side by side on the bed, holdin hands like we wouldn't never let go. I felt like someone had lifted a huge rock off of me, like if I didn't hold on to Zenobia I might float right up to the peak of the ceiling.

We all started to whisper, then we stopped, started up again at the same time, and laughed.

"You first, Lark," Zenobia said. "What happen to you?"

"No, you first," I said. "Last time I saw you he were carryin you into the woods, and I didn't know if I would ever see you again."

Zenobia let go of my hand and scooted acrost the mattress. She leant her back against the wall, her legs drawed up to her chest, her good arm wrapped round them.

"I cain't right remember all the happenins," she said. "First I thought I were dead, next you yank my arm and something big and heavy fall on me. Next I know he is helpin me"—Zenobia pointed to the boy—"and carryin me into the woods like a sack of cotton. Lark, this here's Brightwell, you met him a few days ago, but not by name. He's our friend."

Brightwell nodded.

I looked him in the eye and said, "Thank you for savin Zenobia, but you near scairt me to death when you was talkin at me and tauntin me like a haint. I didn't know who or what you was."

Brightwell shrugged his shoulders. "Sorry, Lark. First when you was talkin I couldn't help but tease you, but then, when you sounded scairt, I knowed I needed to get Zenobia."

I forgave him right quick. And hadn't he taken a beatin from them slave traders and never told them I were hidin right above them in the tree? I owed him somethin fierce.

Brightwell reached inside his shirt and tugged out my old Hannah doll. He passed her to me, and I held her to my heart.

"I never thought to see her again," I said, chokin back my tears.

I glanced from him to Zenobia. "Why, she looks better than she's ever looked."

"Auntie Theodate nursed Brightwell, me, you, and Hannah," Zenobia said. "Auntie takes care of peoples who need her help."

"Who is Auntie Theodate?"

"Lark, you come to her house. You come here three nights ago when you was so sick you couldn't hardly walk, but you found her, found us." Zenobia swiped at a tear with the back of her good hand.

I set quiet for a minute and thought about that night,

but I couldn't rightly remember what had made me come to Auntie's house.

"Are we trapped here?" I asked.

"No, we safe, but it's a long, long story we can talk about tomorrow with Auntie," Brightwell said. "Auntie and some of her family showed me that there are good white folks. We got real friends here, and they has helped people north to a safe place. A free life."

The night I had made my way here flashed into my memory. I had been sick, burnin up with fever.

"Lark, I told you to look for signs to a safe place. You done it. You follered the signs and found your way here," Brightwell said.

I remembered stubbin my toe on a gravestone and then the yellow light from the two windows of the little cabin shinin out at me. I remembered holdin on to the pickets of a fence, one by one, hollyhocks like tall ghosts. I remembered a huge pot over a wicked orange fire.

I remembered Brightwell's words afore he left with Zenobia: "Look for a sign." Then I remembered the twig arrows and the lines of shiny white pebbles.

"Was it you left them signs for me?"

"Lark," Brightwell said, "we slaves, we never tell most folk about the signs. Never tell a white folk. Ever. I were goin to leave you signs, but couldn't set Zenobia down again and again. Hurt her too bad. I were tryin to sign you when Asa come up. He scare us at first, but he talk and we knowed he would help us. He left you signs, and he made sure we got here safe and that you be safe."

Thump, thump, thump. Loud sounds came from somewhere below.

Brightwell raised his finger to his mouth. "The signal," he whispered.

We didn't move, just held hands, squeezin tighter and tighter as heavy steps come up toward us.

Knock three times and call up the devil.
Knock four times and chase him back.

The thumpin stopped. Below us we could hear loud talkin and yellin, and the drawn-out yodel of a hound. Then we heard the sounds of tappin on the wall.

Loud talk again, and then heavy stompin. Tappin again, right close, from the wall at the foot of my bed.

Tap, tap, tap. Then the sound and feel of some-one walkin on the floorboards just the other side of the bricks.

I reached over to the table and knocked soundlessly four times to chase the evil away. As I pulled back my hand, my knuckle hit the side of the cup; it tipped and rolled toward the edge of the table, and water spilt onto the floor. I caught the cup just afore it fell, but the water pooled, then disappeared into the crack between the floor and the trapdoor.

It turned quiet. So quiet that all I heard was the roarin inside my head. I held on to the cup with one hand, Brightwell with the other, and looked over at Zenobia. She had her eyes all squinched together, and sweat run down her forehead and along her nose. Brightwell stared straight ahead, never blinked, never moved; it were like he had fallen deep asleep with his eyes wide open.

"Where'd this water come from?" my pa yelled.

I felt like I always did when Pa come for me at home. I wanted to run, find a tall tree and climb up and out of his sight, but I were stuck in a small room just a few feet above him.

We could hear a voice answer softly.

Pa growled, "Bad roof, bad house."

Another answer, but so soft we couldn't hear the words.

I started to shakin and set the cup back onto the table afore I dropped it. Pa's voice, that voice that scairt me more than a kick or a hittin, it near sent me to the floor.

I could hear more yellin and howlin. Were Pa goin to find his way up here—find me, find Zenobia and Brightwell? I wrapped my arms around myself like I were freezin cold. But I weren't cold, I were scairt, just scairt to my bones and knowin what would happen if he tried to see where that water come from.

Below us a door slammed hard, and the sounds of men and dogs faded.

I still held on to myself, as if I could keep all the scairt inside and all the bad outside.

A few minutes passed afore Brightwell blinked and said, "I think they gone now."

Zenobia let out a long sigh, stood up, and paced two steps down the little room and two steps back, wipin her forehead with the back of her hand, then dryin it on her skirt.

"That time they too close," she whispered. "They come all the way to the attic. Why they keep comin here? Is somebody lettin on that Auntie's is a safe house?"

I could feel myself shakin, but I didn't want Zenobia and Brightwell to see me scairt.

I pushed myself up, set back down, and explained that the shakin were because I'd been so sick.

Zenobia and Brightwell didn't disagree, but they passed a look between them that told me they knew how scairt I were.

I'm right used to takin care of myself. I'm used to knowin where to find a safe place to hide, and to knowin where I can wild gather enough victuals to last for a few days. But here I set—somewhere, and not knowin nothin about where I were or how I'd get away if Pa got close again.

"Zenobia, I need you to catch me up on what is happenin—and where am I?"

Zenobia paced another couple steps and set down beside me.

"We was waitin for you to find your way here. Auntie knowed you were comin."

"After you faint, Auntie let us out of our hidin spot and ask me to carry you up to her room," Brightwell said. "Auntie clean you and dress you in a nightshirt."

"Me and Brightwell snuck outside and burn your clothes under the big soap pot—they was tore up some bad and had your smell all over them."

Zenobia stopped talkin, reached into her pocket, and pulled somethin out.

"Here, Lark," she said. "You needs your good luck. I pulled it out of your pocket afore we burnt them clothes."

My heart jumped. I don't know why, but just curlin my fingers around that buckeye's smooth made me feel right settled inside.

Brightwell leant forward and the rocker creaked. "Then we had to get you up to this room because we knowed that you couldn't be hid downstairs."

"Who's been feedin me?"

"Auntie make the food and either Zenobia or me bring it up. You never even woke most of the time, but once you had a bad dream, and Zenobia had to quick up here and sing to quieten you."

I remembered thinkin that someone were singin to me. It had been Zenobia.

Thump, thump, thump from below.

Brightwell raised his finger to his mouth again. "The signal," he whispered.

We stopped talkin and did the hardest thing— we waited.

*If a candle burns blue, it is a token of bad luck,
for it indicates the presence of a death sperrit.*

Two rapid taps, then a familiar slidin sound of the trapdoor openin, and a rush of cool air mixed with the smell
of bakin bread.

Brightwell reached down and lifted a tin hog-scraper
candlestick and a pile of clothing onto the table. The
candle burned brightly beside him. Next he bent over
the trapdoor and pulled up a tiny silver-haired woman
in drab brown clothes and a white apron. She reminded
me of a wren, but with eyes the blue of cornflowers. She
weren't no bigger than me.

"Good to see thee awake, sweet girl," the woman said
as she brushed at her apron.

I started a-cryin and couldn't stop. I kept them words, *sweet girl,* tucked into my heart, and I always hoped that I would hear them again someday. Nobody had called me sweet girl since my grandpa had passed.

"Lark, this here's Auntie Theodate," Zenobia said as she reached out to comfort me.

That made it worse. I hardly never cry when I'm alone, but I never cry in front of no one. Until today.

"I owe you for helpin me," I said, wipin at my eyes with the sleeve of my nightshirt.

"Thee doesn't owe me," Auntie answered, "but thee will need to help me with what we're doing here if thy friends are to be free."

"Help? What kind of help?"

"I'm sure thee heard thy father and brothers. They said the dogs led them to my house. I had to invite them to come in, but I told them the dogs must stay outside because of my sick, old tabby cat. I knew if I let the dogs in they would lead them straight up here to thee.

"I asked them to sit and share a bit of food with me, but they told me they didn't want food, they wanted to look through my house. I told them they were welcome to look, but that the only thing they would find would be my nephew Asa and my cat."

"But what if they'd found me—found us?" I asked, looking first at Zenobia, then Auntie and Brightwell.

"Don't worry," Zenobia said. "You in the room above the pantry. Trapdoor hid good in the ceiling. Auntie had the old door to the room bricked off like a chimney. Lots of others found a safe place up here too."

I had so many other questions I wanted to ask Auntie, but afore I could say a word, we heard a scramblin sound from below and up popped the head of the red-haired boy I seen in the woods.

"Asa, thee has put the fright into us," Auntie said. "Now come up here and meet Lark, the girl thee found in the woods."

"He the one who led us to Auntie's," Brightwell said. "I told him you needed a safe house too."

The boy pushed himself up through the door, and Brightwell pulled him the rest of the way into the little room, which were crowded as our spring henhouse.

"And you threw them rocks at me?" I asked.

"Thee was startin off the wrong way, and I needed to set thee on the path to Auntie's house. Thee was lookin sick and walked around in a big circle. I needed to wake thee up, but I couldn't stay behind to guide thee. I had to make sure Brightwell and Zenobia made it safe to Auntie's."

"You woke me up all right. You landed them rocks right on my back. But I wouldn't have found my way here without the arrows and the lines of pebbles you left for me."

Asa grinned and stuck out his hand. I reached out, shook it, and said, "You had me right scairt when I saw you with all them men and dogs. I thought you'd send them my way, but you pointed the other way and off they went. They was so close to catchin me, well, I almost climbed down out of the tree to wait for them."

"Thy pa and brothers were even closer today," Asa said. "My father was on a night run with two slaves. Father usually can keep the catchers at bay, but this time it was up to me. I had to keep the dogs away with some of Auntie's soup bones. Sorry, Auntie. I used them most all up. Thy pa had a right hard time getting the dogs to leave here."

We all laughed, and then Auntie pushed the pile of folded clothes toward me.

"Take thy time, Lark. When thee feels fit enough to join us, we will tell thee our plan for moving Zenobia and Brightwell to the North."

My friend Zenobia would be leavin me? Leavin me forever and goin north? I didn't want to help her leave me. I just found her again.

"And we need to find thee a safe house farther away until thy father stops searching," Auntie said.

Auntie didn't know it yet, but I were not lettin Zenobia and Brightwell leave me behind. And I knowed my pa— nothin would stop him huntin for me. He didn't care a goose feather what I wanted or how I were treated, but he did care that I weren't there slavin for him anymore. He counted on me for work, work fittin for a man, not a girl. I belonged to him, like his huntin dogs and his guns. He wouldn't never give up lookin for me around here. No way

I'd wait for him to find me. Safe house or not. Wherever Zenobia went, I were follerin.

A warm breeze whispered through the slats above us. The candle on the table guttered, wavered, and burned blue—the bad death light of sperrits. Brightwell cupped his hand around the flame till it steadied, and the light burnt golden again.

I set back against the wall, plumb wore out, then fingered acrost my buckeye and set it on the table. I couldn't even think anymore about the close call we had or what needed doin in the next few days.

"Thee must rest now, Lark. Zenobia will bring thee a meal. Stay up here until she comes. Take time. Talk. Tomorrow will be here soon," Auntie said.

Auntie helped me and Hannah doll slip under the light summer counterpane that smelt of lavender. She pulled it up to my chin and tucked it around us. When she brushed the wisps of hair off my forehead and patted me, I wanted to curl up against her like a kitten.

"Sleep, sweet girl," Auntie whispered.

I closed my eyes and their voices moved in and out of my dreams. I heard the words *Yardley, white pebbles, twigs,* and then the voices faded. I felt warm inside and out. Like I were all wrapped up in safe for the first time since Grandpa was took. Were this like being in a family?

"Brother Yardley will be thy conductor, Zenobia. Thee

can expect him soon. Say thy good-byes to Lark," Auntie said.

I couldn't open my eyes, couldn't speak. What did Auntie mean, conductor? Good-byes? I would be follerin Zenobia. I would be follerin.

*Never sit when fishing or settling
an important matter or you will
be sitting on your good luck.*

I woke, stretched my arms above my head, and yawned. This were the first time in days I felt like myself. I scooted off the bed, picked up the neat stack of clothes, and dressed. Real clothes, clean clothes, and a pair of brown shoes. I couldn't remember when I last put on a pair of shoes.

Auntie had told me to stay in my room until Zenobia come with food, but I felt caged. How long since I'd been out of this room? I bent over, pushed the rug out of the way, and slid open the trapdoor. I set at the edge of the openin, dangled my bare feet over the side, and listened for sounds. Below me I could see a thin yellow crack of light along the sides of a door. Where did the door lead? My heart beat faster. Should I go down or stay and wait for Zenobia like Auntie asked? My feet wiggled in the air, then brushed against somethin solid. I held on to the edge of the openin, stepped back, and slowly began to climb my way down what weren't steps, but the shelves in a pantry. I felt for another shelf-step, stretched my foot down, and held on. I were starin straight into jars of jam, bottles of preserves, labeled tins of flour and cornmeal, and a bucket of lard.

What would happen when I got downstairs? Would I be brave enough to go through the door? What if someone bad were there? Maybe I should go back up and wait like I was spost to, but curiosity kept a-bitin at me like fleas on a dog, and I couldn't sit still.

Just for a moment, I thought. Just for a moment. I'd go down, maybe peek out the door and try to see what kind of place I were in. My fingers slipped and I swayed backward but caught onto the shelf afore I fell. Three jars toppled over, and afore I could stop it, one dropped to the floor and shattered. The narrow door swung open and the pantry brightened.

"Yi!" I yelled as a pair of hands grabbed me from behind and swung me through the air and onto a clear spot on the floor.

"Lark, you shouldn't never come down without someone givin you the signal," Brightwell said, shakin his finger at me. "You could walk straight into strangers come to buy Auntie's soaps, or worse yet, your pa, or, or a slave trader."

"Sorry, Brightwell. I should've waited, but it's been so long since I been anywhere, and I were just wonderin. . . ."

"Wonderin can lead you to a mess of trouble. You here now. Might as well go out and see Auntie. She thought you might could be comin down for supper, but she didn't know you'd come down so soon—and without the signal."

He lifted me up and hauled me through the door and into the middle of a kitchen bright with the light from a fireplace big enough for Brightwell to stand in. A huge iron pot hung from a crane over the flames. Whatever were cookin smelt like heaven.

When Auntie heard us comin, she lit an oil lamp, carried it to the table, and piled more logs under the pot bubbling above the flames.

"I go pick up the pieces," Brightwell said as he set me down and turned back to the mess I'd made.

"Welcome, Lark. Thee must be hungry. Did thee sleep well?" Auntie asked. She passed a platter of food to Zenobia, who were settin the table.

My tongue got all twisted up and I mumbled an apology for all the ruckus, the broke crockery, the mess, and comin down when I weren't yet called.

Auntie just looked at me and smiled. She were a right patient woman.

A handsome gray tabby cat were curled up on a pile of kindlin in a big, shiny brass applesauce pot beside the fireplace. She never opened her eyes but flicked her ears back and forth as though she wanted to hear every word we said.

My stomach rumbled, and I sniffed at the sweet-smellin food like a rabbit in a field of clover. The table were set with four plates, a platter of big golden biscuits, ham, butter beans, poke sallet, and a bowl mounded with a cloud of grits. A feast.

Auntie pulled out a mule-ear chair crisscrossed with a seat of woven rush. She patted at it and motioned for me to sit. Zenobia perched on a little stool, and Auntie Theodate set on another. Brightwell, so tall he nearly touched the low kitchen ceiling, stooped as he walked acrost the room and checked the big iron latch on the door.

I had so many questions to ask, but I were hungry, and without ever thinkin about manners, reached acrost the table for a biscuit.

Auntie looked at me, her blue eyes twinklin, and grasped Zenobia's good hand, then mine—the one without the biscuit. Brightwell walked over to join us.

"Sit thee down, son." Auntie nodded to a bench beside me.

"Cain't sit tonight, thank you, Auntie—if I do, I be sittin on my good luck, gots to keep it free."

Auntie closed her eyes and bowed her head. Brightwell bowed his and took Zenobia's hand first, then mine after I dropped the biscuit onto my plate.

We were a circle of quiet.

I kept waitin for someone to say the blessin. I opened one eye, tilted my head sideways, and looked around the table. All their heads was down, but nary a word come out of any mouth. Should I pray? Was they waitin on me to do it?

Auntie squeezed my hand, then let it go.

"We Quakers do silent prayers," she said, "just as we do in our First Day meeting."

I'd heard about Quakers and their meetins and some of their strange ways from the preacher's wife. "What kind of meetin can you have without no talkin?" I asked.

Zenobia giggled, took a gulp of milk, and licked the foam off her lips. Auntie explained that they call their day of worship First Day instead of Sunday, and when they gather at their church, they call it a meetin, but without a preacher or words.

I didn't care what they called their churchgoin or how they prayed; I just wanted to put some real, hot food into my mouth. My stomach growled so loud that Auntie laughed and passed me a platter of meat, then the bowl of steamin white grits.

Rain began to fall steady-like.

"Good to have the rain again tonight," Auntie said. "Neither dogs nor travelers will be about on a night like this."

Her words made me feel safer, made me enjoy the tastes, the smells, the dancin firelight even more.

Between bites, Auntie asked us questions about our

lives. I never knowed how hard it would be to hear them stories Brightwell and Zenobia told—and here I thought my life had been bad.

The big tabby cat jumped down from her bed of kindlin and rubbed her softness against my leg. I stretched out my bare foot and smoothed it over the cat's back.

Brightwell told how his ma were taken out of their cabin one night, dragged by her hair so as not to leave any marks on her, and never seen again.

He'd tried to stop the traders, but they kicked him, knocked out his front tooth, beat him till he nearly bit off his tongue, then threw him into the filth of a hog pen.

"My brothers and sisters all screamin for their ma, but she gone, just like our pa. Lord, she gone forever, and I couldn't do nothin to help her. What kind of man am I?" Tears run down his face.

He stopped talkin, shook his head, and said, "I cain't tell no more. It eats me all inside till I feel like a dried-out gourd. Sometimes, when I think on it, I feels . . . tastes the poison runnin through me, eatin through me, fillin my mouth with sick. Minds me that I weren't good as an animal to them people—and times, when I think on that, I gets so mad that I feel like I could kill someone, and then I ain't no more than an animal." He bowed his head and didn't look up.

Zenobia began to talk, lookin straight ahead, never blinkin. "The men, they makes me eat the tobacca worms that I missed on them plants. They shove them big green worms into my mouth, down my throat till I near choke. I fight back, so they laugh, then they string me up high on the big tree to punish me for fightin. I there, hangin till my wrists are burnin fire." She held out her twisted, scarred wrists. "Then they stake me down on the anthill. They laugh, laugh, while them ants crawl all over me, in my eyes, in my nose, down my throat, stingin me, stingin me, till I were on fire. I member me screamin, screamin, and they laughin and laughin. I knows how Brightwell feels. If I could've right then, why, I think I would've picked up a gun and killt them all."

Both Auntie and I wiped at tears. Then Auntie looked from Brightwell to Zenobia.

"Children," she said, "thee must remember what we Friends believe. Thee cannot overcome evil with violence, nor violence with evil, elstwise thee will be like thine enemy."

Brightwell and Zenobia told more stories until my heart and my insides was all twisted and torn as her wrists. Even with my eyes squeezed closed the pictures of all them horrors come into me. I wanted to retch.

"I don't know how we could ever be that bad, as bad as our enemies," I said. "I do know that I'll do whatever— whatever it takes to help you get to free soil." I promised myself that I wouldn't never let them bad things happen to them again.

"Free soil. Freedom," Zenobia said. "Nobody tearin our families into pieces, work a good job, hold up our heads like peoples."

Brightwell nodded in agreement and said, "Ummm-hmm. No white folks tearin our families into pieces, work a good job, ummm-hmm, hold up our heads like peoples."

He paced back and forth, starin at the emptiness between me and Zenobia.

"Sometimes I think I be tore in so many pieces I ain't never gonna be a real man. How you fix yerself when you're tore at and tore at again and again?"

I thought about how I mended my skirt and my pa's and brothers' clothes, and how I darned socks and stitched together old Hannah doll from all the tore-up pieces of my mama's wore-out quilts.

"You just keep mendin and darnin, stitchin and stitchin. At first, things look all pieced together, but after a while, you don't even notice the stitched-up spots everywhere; they just look all of a piece. Never like new, but all of a piece and good enough to last a life," I said.

Brightwell looked down at me, his pacin stopped.

"Then I best start piecin myself back together. Me and Zenobia have a new life comin on quicker than leaf drop, and we want to be near good as we can be."

They deserved their new lives, but I couldn't—no, wouldn't—let them to go without me.

Auntie rose and told us that we all needed to rest. We

carried our plates to a bucket, righted up the kitchen, then stood in a small circle holdin on to each other.

"Tomorrow I show you where we hidin," Zenobia said. "Too late tonight."

We hugged; then Zenobia and Brightwell, candlesticks in hand, opened a small door and closed it behind them.

"Rest well, sweet girl," Auntie said.

I walked acrost the kitchen, turned around to drink in all the peace inside that small room, then walked into the pantry.

Auntie stood below me as I crawled up the shelf-stairs.

"Thee must close the door tightly so the opening won't show. Oh, and, sweet girl, please don't come down tomorrow till we signal thee."

"Sorry, Auntie, but thank you for tonight and for everythin."

I pulled myself through the trapdoor, slid it back into place, and settled the rug atop it.

My nightshirt were on the bed, but I pushed it aside and crawled on top of the counterpane. I watched the light from the candle as it shone bright, then soft, then bright again.

I slipped off the bed, knelt, and bowed my head, prayin for a better life for Brightwell and Zenobia and askin that Auntie and Asa be kept safe. Somethin inside me wanted to ask for a better life, a safe life, for me too, but I remembered that travelin preacher sayin that you should always pray with an open heart for others. Never for yerself. But that preacher didn't say nothin about me prayin to my mama.

"Mama," I whispered. "Mama, won't you help lead me to a better life? I promise I'll always help others afore myself. Thank you, Mama."

I crawled back up onto my narrow bed and reached acrost the table to rub at the smooth of my buckeye. The little room were so crammed with life earlier today, but now it felt lonely, so lonely, and sad.

I blew out the candle. The warm black closed around me, and I pulled my Hannah doll up against my heart. The floors of the old house creaked and cracked. Grandpa always told that a crackin house was a sure sign of death comin. I could feel the chicken skin risin on my arms.

Outside I heard the loud calls of crickets, frogs, and a bird, trillin over and over—the sounds of a safe summer night.

Then silence. Silence thick and dark.

Were somebody outside watchin Auntie's house?

*Lightning accompanied by a thunderbolt produces
a madstone. Find one and keep it in your pocket
to protect yourself from lightning, or put it in your house
by a chimney and your home will never be hit.*

I laid in bed listenin for the night sounds to start up, but they didn't. Then the rain began again, fallin gentle on the roof, then harder, poundin and poundin, then soft again, drummin lightly like fingertips on a tin bucket. That were the last I remember afore the saw-sound crowin of a rooster and three loud thumps woke me. A gray mornin barely lit the room.

I rolled to my side and watched as the trapdoor slid back and Zenobia's head poked above the floor.

"Mornin, Lark. This rain good. Nobody out now. No smells of us laid down. Auntie say she felt someone here most of last night, watchin the house." Zenobia's words tumbled together like the water rushin off the edge of the roof.

So I weren't wrong worryin about the quiet out there. Someone had been watchin Auntie's house, lookin for somethin that didn't fit right.

I got up from the bed and reached for Zenobia's good arm. She scrambled into the room and set beside me.

A tray loaded with food appeared right behind her.

"Got it, Lark?" Brightwell asked as he passed the tray up to me.

We heard voices. Brightwell looked down, stepped back, and disappeared below us.

I set the tray on the bedside table and Zenobia set next by me.

"Auntie goin to tell you later tonight where you be goin soon," Zenobia said. "And she give you a fine new name for the travelin. She call you Miss Abigail Harlan, but I likes Lark best." More voices below, and then Brightwell climbed through the door, slid it back into place, and set down in the rockin chair. His long legs, near thick as an oak limb, stretched all the way to the bed.

We could hear the wind gainin outside, the sounds of rain poundin on the roof, and far away a huge clap of thunder, then a long, rollin rumble like the big wheels of a passin wagon. The storm had finally broken the hot spell and the little room felt cool and fresh.

A flash of lightnin shone through the slats above us and lit the top of the wall in brilliant stripes.

"Tonight," Brightwell said, "Yardley and Asa come by and say late tonight we movin on to another stop, but you stayin here, Lark, till you get moved north. Auntie think it's not safe for all three of us to leave together."

"What you mean we're not leavin together?"

Another flash. The room lit for an instant, and I could see every scar on Brightwell's face. I wished I could run outside and find that piece of thunderbolt madstone so's Brightwell, Zenobia, and me could travel safe together.

Zenobia raised a finger to her mouth and cautioned me to quieten down.

"If you're goin, I'm goin," I said over the crash and rumble of another clap, not near as close as the last. Weren't no way I'd let my friends go without me.

"No, Lark. You cain't," Brightwell said. "This be best. Auntie say Friend Yardley can fit two in the hidin place, but he don't have no room for three of us. And your pa's dogs knows your smell. They could find you most anywhere. Auntie and her brother still tryin to piece out how to move you from here."

"Where you goin?" I asked, lookin from one to the other.

"We goin to Philadelphia to meet a Mr. Still and a conductor, then north to the Promised Land," Zenobia said.

Promised Land? Did that mean heaven?

"But what about me?" I asked. "Where will I go for a new life? Won't we always be friends like we promised?"

"We always be friends," said Zenobia, "even if we never

see each other again—just like my family always be my family, even if I never find them again. You white, Lark. You'll be Miss Abigail Harlan. You gots a better chance to find your freedom."

I couldn't think on that. I would not let them leave me behind.

The food set on the tray, and though I hungered, I couldn't take a bite. I felt like a huge lump of earth laid right in the middle of my stomach and filled it up to my heart.

If you hear a chicken sneeze at three in the morning,
you'll be awake until the sun rises,
and you'll lie awake the next night.

After dark, Brightwell disappeared through the trap-door and backed down the pantry shelf-steps. Zenobia and me both leant over and watched him open the narrow door and put his eye up against the bright crack of light.

"C'mon down. All safe," he said as he reached up, grabbed our waists one at a time, and swung us to the floor.

When we walked through the pantry door, the warm kitchen welcomed us. Auntie walked back and forth carryin food to the table and callin for her cat to come for supper.

We set down together and held hands, and tonight I knew what to do. We said our silent prayer and then began our meal.

Between bites we talked—nothin about what was goin to happen durin the night, nothin about us never seein each other again; we just talked about the North and the peoples who had made a new life there. Some of them, with the help of others, were slowly findin family they thought to never see again and helpin to move them north too.

"Just a few years ago thee would have found shelter in Pennsylvania, New York, Ohio, any number of places, but not now—not with the Fugitive Slave Act. Now the slave traders and marshals can hunt runaways anywhere in the country and return them to their owners," Auntie said as she passed a board of bread to me.

"Maybe someday, after I work and make some savins, maybe I can find my ma and papa and my baby sister," Zenobia said. "Move them to the Promised Land to have a free life too."

I didn't know where she would begin to look, but if anyone could find someone, I knowed it would be Zenobia.

By the time we'd ate our supper and washed the dishes, I couldn't feel no more sorrow. I were so tired I could barely stand, barely talk, but Brightwell and Zenobia wanted to show me their hidin spots afore we all went to sleep.

Brightwell walked to a small door acrost the room, opened it, and picked up a candlestick. The three of us made our way down the steep steps and into a cellar that smelt of beeswax, lavender, roses, and sage.

"Them smells so powerful," said Brightwell, "there ain't a dog nowheres that could sniff us out down here."

Thick bars of soap set curin on tall shelves that lined the walls. Dozens of pairs of candles, joined together by white wickin, hung over a long rack fitted with wooden rungs. The windowless cellar with its stone-cobbled floor were cool as an autumn mornin.

Zenobia walked to the tall shelf on the right side of the room. She reached high behind the wooden framework, slid her hand down, and moved her finger back and forth against something.

Snap. The shelf slowly opened.

Inside a cubbyhole cut into the stone walls of the foundation were a thick pallet, some blankets, and a pillow. The space were just big enough for Zenobia to lie down.

Brightwell showed me his hideout behind the other shelf. It were bigger than Zenobia's and his pallet bristled with straw. He patted it and said, "One more night on this, then we on to find free soil."

He would find his free soil, but he wouldn't be findin it without me.

Brightwell and Zenobia said good night as we hugged, three of us at once, lingerin, as though we could hold on to this time forever. Then they turned, and without lookin back, crawled into their little hidin spots and pulled the shelves closed.

I climbed upstairs, shut the cellar door, and looked around for Auntie. She come from the small bornin room beside the kitchen and motioned for me to foller her.

Auntie walked over to a bucket bench by the side of the fireplace, lifted a loose board in the seat, and pointed inside.

"Here is a sack of food. This hidden pouch has thy knife, a letter, and some money," she said as her tiny hands flew across each piece like birds on the wing. "Here is a medicine kit, more clothes, and high shoes."

I fingered through the clothes, found Grandpa's knife hid in a side pouch, and looked over to Auntie.

"What's happenin, Auntie? Am I leavin? Why is all this here for me?"

Auntie just patted at me. "I will explain more to thee tomorrow, Lark. Thee must be ready for anything," she said quietly. "Thee must listen to the night. Read it well. This time thee mustn't move out of thy hiding place no matter what happens. I'll give thee the signal when it is safe to come down."

She walked acrost the room, pecked a small kiss on my cheek, and bent to stroke her sleepin cat.

I reached up to the spot where her lips had touched on me—two years since Grandpa passed, two years since I'd felt a kiss—then walked into the pantry and climbed the shelf-stairs. The trapdoor slipped silently into place. When I looked around at the little room, it felt like safe to me, like what I thought a home might be.

I started to take off my clothes, but then thought the better of it. What if I needed to leave fast? I pulled off my shoes and set them beside my narrow bed, pinched the wick of the sputterin candle, and stretched out with Hannah doll beside me. Although I didn't think I could still myself enough to sleep, I did, and without a dream.

❧

I slept hard but woke to a loud sound. What was it? Did the chicken sneeze and wake me? I set up and stared into the dark, makin sure not to settle into the creakin spot in the middle of the bed. Then come noises and voices downstairs.

Were Yardley come to pick up Zenobia and Brightwell?

I slid off the bed and laid on the floor, put my ear to the trapdoor, and listened so hard I sweared I could hear the Catoctin Crick ragin inside me. Then come screamin and the sound of shoutin, dogs a-barkin, and the crash of pottery. Then come nothin.

*Rob a cat of one of its nine lives and
your own will be shortened by half.*

How long I laid there listenin I cain't say. I kept my
ear on the trapdoor but never moved for fear of missin a
sound or makin a sound.

I wanted to slide the door open and climb down, but
Auntie's warnin not to move out of my room no matter
what happened kept me nailed to the floor.

A noise come, and then the sound of the pantry door
openin.

The thunder bucket were too far away to reach. I set
up, inched toward the table, and grabbed the pitcher of
water.

Knock, knock, knock.

The trapdoor moved slowly. I set there, pitcher in hand, wonderin if somebody had learnt of our signal.

"Lark," a familiar, hushed voice called. "Lark."

The trapdoor slid open and Asa's red head appeared. His big green eyes darted around the little room and back to me.

"Brightwell and Zenobia aren't with thee? Where's Auntie? What happened? The house is all torn apart," Asa said, his voice shakin.

"Did you check the hidin spots behind the shelfs?" I asked.

Asa nodded. "They're empty, and it looks like there was a fight down there."

"I don't know what happened," I said. "I stayed put just like Auntie told me to. Now I'm goin to find out." I stuffed my lucky buckeye into my pocket and Hannah doll into my rough shirt. I didn't bother to pull on the shoes, just tossed them through the trapdoor and heard them thunk as they hit the floor.

"No, Lark, thee mustn't leave until I find out where Auntie is and who was here. Father is coming home today; he'll help us."

"I'm better off doin than not doin. I cain't sit not knowin what happened to my friends. We got to find out and help them."

Asa shrugged his shoulders. "Thee knows what thee must do, but let's make some plans so's we don't walk right into trouble."

I dropped my legs over the edge of the door and moved my foot until I found the first shelf-step in the pantry, then backed down.

Asa follered and with one hand slid the trapdoor closed behind us. I looked up. The door disappeared seamlessly into the planks of the ceiling.

Asa reached the floor just a second after me. I pushed open the pantry door and looked around. Everythin had changed. I pulled on the shoes and we stepped into Auntie's little kitchen, all tore apart, like a storm had blowed through. Had it ever been filled with candlelight and friends? The fireplace set dark and cold. Splintered chairs, stools, and benches; broken plates and kindlin covered the floor. The big applesauce pot that belonged beside the fireplace set upside down.

Meeooooww.

Asa and I looked around the room and tried to find where the feeble sound come from.

Meeeooooooowww. Louder now.

"Aw, it's Moses," Asa said. "She's somewhere hiding."

I picked my way slowly acrost the room, every step crunchin on broken pottery. Asa come behind me and reached to bolt the door, but the latch were gone, broken off by someone forcin into the house. He grabbed a heavy bench, dragged it to the front of the door, and tilted it on end and at an angle to wedge it closed.

My eyes couldn't stop movin, takin in every corner of

the room, searchin for signs, lookin toward the window where the curtain once hung.

Meeooooowww, again. We was close.

"Where is she?" I asked.

Asa walked to the big applesauce pot and turned it right side up.

Rrraaal. Moses cat sprang from under the pot and disappeared through the open cellar door, leavin a trail of bright-red paw prints behind her.

"We have to help her," I said, "afore we go we have to tend her wounds for Auntie. She's all the family Auntie has."

"No, Lark. Auntie's family is as big as Virginia. Why, her family is bigger than Virginia. She has family everywhere, and they're all alive because of her." His green eyes welled with tears. "But we do have to help Moses. Auntie loves her. The healing salves and herbs are over there," he said as he pointed acrost the kitchen.

"Moses is stubborn and ornery," Asa said. "I'll go get her."

He disappeared into the darkness of the sweet-smellin cellar.

"Moses!" he called. "Moses, come on out and we'll fix thee up right good. Moses, come on out now."

Familiar bunches of healin herbs hung from the beams, and small tins and pots perched along the shelf.

I reached for the thick green bunch of hairy comfrey, a

handful of plantain's tongue-shaped leaves, some arnica, and a tin of dried golden calends flowers.

Asa reappeared with Moses cradled in his arms. The cat's head hung, her eyes open but filmy and lifeless. Looked to me she were hurt so bad it would surely shorten the life of whoever done this.

"Can thee help her?" Asa asked, holdin her out toward me.

A bloody cut acrost the cat's side dipped into the light gray fur of her belly and stained it the pink of Mama's old roses.

"This is one way I can repay Auntie for all she done for me," I said as I laid Moses cat on the table.

"Auntie never wants repaying, Lark. Doing is good enough for her."

I pushed my long braids behind my ears and tied them together in a knot, then bent over Moses.

"Asa, get me some water, please, and some of Auntie's vinegar, and clean rags so's I can bind her."

He walked to the window, quickly looked outside, then slid the latch of the dry-sink door and lifted out some neatly folded sackcloth and a crockery jug of vinegar.

"You're lucky Moses isn't awake. She can be wild and mean if she's hurt or sick," Asa said as he tacked a dish-cloth against the window.

"How'd she ever get herself a name like Moses?" I asked. I glanced around the kitchen lookin for shadows, listenin for anythin that meant trouble.

I slowly worked my fingers through the cat's thick fur. Asa lifted the big teakettle from the crane in the fireplace and poured water and vinegar into what looked like the one remaining unbroken bowl.

Moses laid stretched out and never moved. I cleaned a deep gash in her side and belly, and half a dozen smaller wounds told the tale of dogs.

"Moses is named after a Maryland slave woman who ran herself to freedom in Pennsylvania. She called it the Promised Land." Asa bent toward the cat and laid his hand between her ears.

"Moses thought freedom was all she needed, but it was bitter to her till she could share it. So she turned around and headed back to save others. Think on that. She went south when every slave trying to escape headed north."

"Who is she?" I asked as I cleaned another one of Moses's cuts.

"Her name is Harriet Tubman, but her nickname is Moses. Nobody knows how many slaves she's led to freedom."

I knew that name. I were scairt of her. When we was in town, I seen a broadside posted in Purcell's Store that said she were "dangerous and a threat to slave owners' rights." It showed a picture of a small Negra woman with a dent in the middle of her forehead and a scarred-up neck. That picture didn't look scary, but the words about her was.

The poster said that if you caught her the reward were a thousand dollars. A thousand dollars. The most money

I'd ever seen all at once were ten dollars, and that near took the breath from me. I couldn't believe there could be a thousand dollars anywhere or that anyone would pay that much money just to capture one little woman.

Now I knowed better. She weren't dangerous, and she weren't just one little woman. She were Harriet Tubman, Moses, and she were brave as I wanted to be, but braver than I ever could be.

The cat twitched. I rinsed the deepest cut with the vinegar and water, then laid on a handful of wet knit bone, arnica, plantain, and boneset mixed with calends. Carefully, gently, I wound strips of clean sackcloth around Moses's body to hold the poultice in place. As I worked I sang:

> "When Israel was in Egypt's Land,
> Let my people go!
> Oppressed so hard they could not stand,
> Let my people go!
> Go down, Moses,
> Way down in Egypt's land;
> Tell old Pharaoh
> To let my people go!
> No more shall they in bondage toil,
> Let my people go!"

I stroked Moses's fur, smoothed it back into place, and run my fingers over her side. "I'll change the poultice again afore I leave tonight."

Asa picked up a small rug and made a bed for Moses on top of the bench by the window. I carried her acrost the kitchen and settled her into place. She laid still—still as well water.

"Thee can't leave tonight without my father and me," Asa said.

"We need to foller their trail till we find them."

Them. I couldn't say the names. Auntie. Brightwell. Zenobia. It hurt my heart just thinkin them.

From outside on the front porch come shoutin and the sound of boots poundin up the steps, pushin and pushin at the door until the bench shifted and began a slow slide down the wall.

"The cellar," Asa said, "the cellar. No time for the attic."

I turned and run down the steep stairs into darkness.

*Beware: misfortunes
come in sets of three.*

The cellar, lit by a square of light from the kitchen, were my only hope. I didn't dare close the door behind me for fear of stumblin into somethin and never findin my way into one of the hideouts.

My hands touched the edge of a shelf, and I felt for the latch. I tugged, slipped my hand down the side, fingerin and pushin, but nothin moved. Why hadn't I paid more attention to how Zenobia got it open when I had the chance?

"Who's out there?" I heard Asa shout, but I couldn't take time to look back.

I started again at the top of the shelf, slidin my hand

down till my finger hit a small latch. *Snap.* The shelf moved an inch, then swung open wide enough for me to slip inside. Just as I stepped into the pure darkness, Asa opened the kitchen door to the outside and the cellar brightened.

I backed in and my hand fumbled against the edge, found a knob, and slowly, so as not to knock over any soaps, I pulled the heavy shelf closed.

My hands patted at the emptiness in front of me and touched the mattress that Zenobia had slept on just a few hours ago. What had she thought and felt when her hopes for freedom were ripped away from her?

Muffled sounds come from the kitchen, but I couldn't make out the words. Then yellin, a heavy thud, and more yellin. Why hadn't I brought Moses cat down with me? I shouldn't have left her behind.

I could hear feet movin through the house. Talkin, the thump of somethin heavy, and the smell of a cheroot bein smoked close by.

My fingers found a wooden knob on the door. I held on as tight as I could in case someone figured out how to open it. But I never moved.

The noises stopped. I waited. And waited. I finally let go of the door, straightened my tired fingers, and laid down on the pallet. When I turned my head toward the stone wall, tiny grains of light, as tiny as the faraway stars in the night sky, shone through chinks in the mortar. It gave me some comfort to see that.

Asa. I worried that he were hurt, but I remembered Auntie's caution about stayin hid, and I knowed that if I got caught there weren't no way I could help Zenobia, or Brightwell, or Auntie. Were my grandpa's words about bad luck always comin in threes provin true? Three souls I wanted to help, but how could one twelve-year-old girl do that? Then I thought of the brave little woman called Moses. She done it all by herself. Step by step, mile by mile. I could do it too.

Tap. Tap. Tap.

The shelf opened and Asa's voice whispered, "All clear, Lark."

I slid off the pallet and stood up. Asa looked more upset than I'd ever seen him. A thin trickle of blood run from the side of his mouth.

"More slave traders came by looking for runaways. I just showed them the rooms and asked them what they thought they could find here after all this," he said, motionin toward the kitchen's mess.

"They said everyone knows this house is on the Underground Railroad. I just told them that the closest railroad was miles away. Then that woman who looks like a man got mad at me for my 'smart talkin' and hit me."

"The woman-man?" I asked, my heart poundin faster.

"Yes, the woman who looks like a man. I saw her out in the woods with Brightwell and some other boys a few days ago. She hurt him right bad. She kept saying that she knew we stole her slave boy and kept her from her reward.

She told me she would break both my legs and beat me like she beat those slaves, and that I'd never steal from her again."

I shook my head. The woman-man. Weren't no way I could ever forget her and how she whipped Brightwell with rawhide as I hid in the tree above them and watched—helpless.

Asa wiped at his mouth. "I watched her beat him. It near killed me. I followed them to their campsite and waited until everyone slept that night. Then I cut Brightwell and the other boy out of their ropes. They both ran away before I could tell them where to hide. Would thee call that stealing?" he asked.

"Oh law, no, Asa. That weren't stealin; that were savin, but it made that woman-man meaner than a cottonmouth." Lord have mercy. I started up the stairs. I had to find Brightwell afore they did—and this time I wouldn't be helpless.

*If graveyard dirt falls on your feet
or your shoes and you don't wipe it off,
you'll soon be put into your own grave.*

Asa closed the shelf and follered me up the stairs to the kitchen. Poor Moses, there she laid on the bench, her rug ripped from beneath her. The poultice set all akilter, and blood were oozin from her side.

"I let you and Auntie down, Moses. I should've taken you to the cellar with me."

The cat's ears flicked back and forth, but her eyes never opened.

I looked around the kitchen afore I set to work. The door were already propped closed. A heavy rope wound from the broken latch and hitched to a thick iron hook buried in the wall.

Asa brought the teakettle over and poured clean water into the bowl. When I dipped the rag into the water and dabbed at the gash, Moses's side rippled in pain.

"Sorry, girl, so sorry, but I have to do this," I said as I repacked the cut with a poultice and bound it to her body.

Asa stood beside me, smoothin at Moses's head and talkin soft to her. "I'll take her over to my house so she will be safe," he said.

"Are you sure your father will be home today?" I asked. "Can't anyone else help us?"

"People are most afraid to help now. Two Friends had their homes seized, and they were run out of town for stealing slaves. Since then people are a mite more cautious."

Asa bent down, picked up the rug and Moses, and stood in front of me. I unwound the rope, pulled it out of the iron loop, and pushed the door open.

"Lark, thee won't be safe here now. Our meetinghouse is just down the road. Thee must change into the clothes Auntie left and take shelter there. As soon as it is dark someone will come with a wagon to move thee north," he said. "Father and I will go after Auntie, Zenobia, and Brightwell."

There weren't no way on this green earth that they was movin me anywhere except on the road to find my friends. We couldn't waste no time now. We had to find them and save them somehow.

"Nobody is movin me north," I said. "Not when my

friends are in trouble. You best come to the meetinhouse and pick me up so's I can help. You don't come for me and I'll go on my own. I couldn't never forgive myself if, if . . ." I didn't even want to think on the bad.

Asa clucked his tongue, shook his head, and walked onto the porch carryin Moses cat like a baby. I looked around the yard to make sure no one were watchin us. When I turned back, Asa had melted into the shadows and disappeared in the trees.

I glanced around the room and walked over to the bucket bench. When I lifted the seat and looked into the hidin spot, I found a store of goods: a fancy new travelin sack, Grandpa's knife, and more clothes—fine, city-girl clothes, colorful as a mallard drake, with a green silk bonnet trailin long ribbons, and soft, black side-button high shoes. A small envelope held a letter introducing me as Abigail Harlan, the daughter of a storekeeper and farmer.

Beneath a thin shimmy laid a paper scribed with the words "Thee must wear these clothes and keep your hair hidden under thy bonnet. Thy father has posted thy description. All are looking for a young red-haired girl. Be safe, sweet girl, and don't be afraid to be hidden in plain sight."

What did Auntie mean, hidden in plain sight? How could I hide when I were drest up like I were goin to meet President Buchanan? I'd have to think on them words.

The door to the bornin room stood open. Auntie's spinnin wheel and work stool set in a pool of late-afternoon sun. Her niddy noddy and skeins of gray and brown yarn hung from pegs. A splint-oak basket set on its side— shears, needles, linen twine, and woven fabric all spilt acrost the floor next by a spiny hetchel. I bent down, scooped everythin back into the basket, and set it aright for Auntie's return.

No more dallyin. I went back to the bucket bench, took off my shoes and rough country clothes, and shook my lucky buckeye out of the pocket. The shimmy slipped down easy over my head. It smelt of Auntie's lavender. I stepped into the fancy dress. My first fine dress. All my clothes was always handed down from my brothers and from the church, but these fit like they'd been made special for me. I run my hands acrost the smooth blue fabric; in my whole life, I had never felt clothes so soft against my skin.

I picked up the fancy shoes, felt the soft leather, and slipped my feet into their tightness. My land, how would I ever be able to climb a tree or run in such? How would I even be able to walk? Step by step. Mile by mile, just like Moses. I dropped my lucky buckeye into my pocket, folded the country clothes neat-like on top of the shoes, and tucked them below Hannah doll in my travelin sack.

Dark were comin on. I picked up Auntie's fresh loaf of bread, some meat, and the last of the summer peaches and stuck them into my sack.

I don't know how I done it, but I untied the door again and opened it for the last time, never lookin backward.

How could I just walk away from the first place that had ever felt like home and family to me? But I had to.

I walked the narrow road to where I come in over a week ago. Straight back along the fence, the tall hollyhocks swayin and starin at me. Past the buryin ground, makin sure not to get any dirt on my shoes so's I wouldn't end up there in the ground too. On toward the long stone meetinhouse standin on a little rise above the town.

I walked up three thick granite steps and tugged at the big double doors, but they didn't move. Was they locked? I pulled again and felt some give on the left door. It shifted, stuck, swolled by the rains, then fought against my tuggin. I pulled harder and the bottom of the door dragged, then scraped against the threshold and creaked open.

Inside, the sweet smell of flowers met me, and somewhere close by the slow *tuck-tuck, tuck-tuck, tuck-tuck* of a clock sounded its heartbeat.

In the dim light, I picked my way up an aisle surrounded on both sides by rows of tall wooden benches.

I settled myself and my sack down on a side bench that faced acrost to another row, stretched my legs, and tried to wiggle my tired toes.

"Mama," I said, "how do folks wear such shoes and get any good walkin done?"

Mama didn't answer, but hearin my voice fill this peaceful place helped me to settle in.

The smell of the bread made me hungry, but supper alone weren't the same as supper with Auntie, Brightwell, and Zenobia. I could see all their faces—Brightwell grinnin at me after he near scairt me to death in my attic room. Zenobia sittin on the big sycamore branch and swingin her long, skinny, heron-bird legs over the crick. Auntie, I could see Auntie's blue eyes twinklin when I reached for the biscuit afore our silent prayer.

"Auntie, Zenobia, Brightwell, how about I keep talkin with you just like I do my mama and grandpa? That would be some good comfort to me, keep me from missin you so much till I find you again."

I felt better already.

Just as I reached for the heel of the bread, I heard a sound. I stopped, listened closely, and then—a slow, dragged-out scrapin and familiar creakin. The door! The door to the meetinhouse were openin. I waited to hear if Asa or his father called out to me, but they didn't. Someone pushed against the stuck door and stepped inside.

If you see the new sickle moon clear,
you will see no trouble while that moon lasts.

I crawled acrost the floor below the bench and pushed the sack ahead of me. When I got to the end of the row, I wedged myself into the tiny space between the bench and the wall and pulled my sack into my lap.

I were pantin like one of our huntin dogs. I pushed my face into the sack and forced myself to close my mouth and breathe slow and quiet.

Step, thump, step, thump, step, thump.

I squeezed my eyes closed.

Tuck-tuck, tuck-tuck, tuck-tuck. Here I were near dyin of fear and the old clock kept on steady.

Step, thump.

Tuck-tuck.

Now I knowed how a rabbit felt. Should I break and run? But how could I run in these shoes?

Step, thump, step, thump.

Tuck-tuck, tuck-tuck.

I opened my eyes and looked acrost the benches and out to the tree brushin its big leaf hands against the glass.

"Who's here?" a man's voice boomed.

I couldn't answer. Wouldn't answer.

Zenobia's face come into my head. Her eyes was open so wide I could see clear to her soul. She were standin in the cellar at my pa's house and gettin ready to climb the ladder and run for it.

"Deer shot when it runs," I'd said to her. But now it were her voice warnin me not to run.

"This is yer last chance. Stand up and show yerself or I'll use the whip."

He waited.

Could he hear my heart a-beatin?

"Show yerself!"

Swoosh. Crack.

Even with my eyes shut I could see that whip slicin through the air.

Did he think that would make me want to show myself?

He walked along the far side of the meetinhouse, tappin at the tops of the benches.

The steps and tappin come louder.

"Where are you?" the man asked. "Where are you?" His voice singsong, wheedlin, like the one my pa and brothers used when they wanted somethin.

"Y'all come on out now. I won't hurt you."

I knew them words and didn't trust them a mite more than I trusted them from my pa's mouth.

The dark settled over me and everythin stopped. It were like the old meetinhouse held its breath, waitin to see what would happen next.

Footsteps again, then *tap, tap, tap.* Wood against wood.

I pulled into myself and tried to be smaller. I wanted to melt into the wall. Disappear.

His heavy footsteps and tappin let me know where he walked.

Now down the side aisle by the big window. Turn. Now along the benches facin each other below the clock. Turn. Now acrost another aisle. Turn. Now up toward me.

I could hear his breathin as he come closer and felt my breath movin in and out, keepin time with his.

Tap, tap, tap.

I almost jumped when I felt-heard him tap on the top of my bench.

Then he turned again. Now the heavy steps moved down the aisle toward where he come in.

The night crowded against the window, the leaves lost in darkness but scratchin loud against the glass.

The man turned, run up to the window, and lifted the sash.

"Dang! She climbed out afore I come in."

He pulled down the window.

Quick footsteps, then the familiar sound of the door arguin against its openin. Then the creak as the door dragged acrost the threshold.

The door slammed closed.

I didn't move.

Tuck-tuck, tuck-tuck.

The leaf hands scratched gently against the window.

The meetinhouse settled back into its old peace, and I could smell the sweet of the flowers again.

I let out my breath and whispered, "Thank you, Mama and Grandpa, thank you, Brightwell, Zenobia, Auntie. Thank you for bein here with me."

My body ached, but I stayed put for a long, long time. My knees felt like they wouldn't never go straight again. Finally, after waitin and listenin, I knew it were safe to move.

I grabbed the smooth, curled end of the bench, braced myself against the wall, and pushed myself up.

My feet, gripin against the pain of the shoes, barely held me.

I picked up the travelin sack and limped to the back door of the meetinhouse. When I pulled the door open and walked outside, the night sounds stopped. The thin sickle of new moon shone through the twisted branches of an oak. I let out my breath. Good luck for me while the moon lasts.

Dark. Quiet. I stood still and let the peace come into me. Then I smelt it. The thick sourness of sweat and the bitterness of whiskey. I knowed that smell.

If a buzzard flies overhead, don't let
him cast his shadow across you or you will have
nothing but bad luck for a fortnight.

The wagon rattled and thundered along the rutted road. My head throbbed, achin so deep inside I couldn't move. I opened my eyes and looked up at the dark night sky. Where were the new sickle moon, and why had my luck run out so fast?

Three bright stars, the ones my grandpa called the three-corner hat, glistered above. I felt some comfort seein how they follered along, lookin down, watchin over me like old friends.

"Grandpa, where am I? Grandpa, the stars." His voice come to me, singin deep from his heart:

Who are these, like stars appearing,
These, before God's throne who stand?
Each a golden crown is wearing:
Who are all this glorious band?

I smelt the familiar smoke of a cheroot and heard the *clop, clop* of horse hooves. The wagon hit a hole and jumped high, then slammed down, rocked, and rumbled on.

"Owww," I moaned, holdin the sides of my head to keep it from movin. When the road smoothed, I let go. My hands felt sticky and wet. I held them under my nose—they smelt of blood. No wonder my head hurt.

I wiped my hands on a pile of dirty straw. I sure didn't want to get no blood on my fine new dress. Then I reached up to brush wisps of hair off my face. My bonnet, where were my bonnet? I remembered Auntie's caution to keep my hair covered. I tried to sit up, but the pure pain of it kept me down.

When I moved my hand acrost the rough wooden bed of the wagon, it run into the soft edge of my fancy green bonnet. I pulled it toward me, lifted my head, and slipped it over my hair. Just doin that took most all my might.

I woke again, my head still hurtin. Night had run to dawn, and long wisps of pink mares' tails streaked the sky. Sunrise soon.

Sleep come again, sleep, hurtin, and a mess of dreams about Zenobia and me runnin, runnin, always a-runnin.

A big jolt shook me awake. It hurt some to open my eyes onto the clear sky and the sun burnin bright and hot on my face. My head felt like someone were tryin to split it open with a maul.

Hurtin or not, I'd spent about as much time as I could lyin down. I turned onto my stomach and looked up at a big, thick man with wide shoulders and long, dirty gray hair. Twin streams of bad-smellin smoke curled behind him.

How had he found me? Where were he takin me?

I poked my head above the rail and saw half a dozen wagons stopped in the shade of trees. Horses drank in a lazy crick, so shallow it didn't make a whisper.

Five other wagons stood nearby in the full meanness of the summer sun. Shackled and tied to the sides of the wagons were Negra men, women, and children. Some cried; others paced in small circles till there were a rut worn into the dusty ground. Were Zenobia and Bright-well somewhere in the crowd?

I set up slow-like, brushed at my dress, and tucked a wisp of hair under my bonnet. Time to forget about the hurtin and start tryin to think out what I were goin to do. Was Yardley and Asa somewhere behind, follerin on our trail? What if they didn't find us? I couldn't hope that anyone else would or could save me from this scrambled-up mess of trouble.

"Whooa!" the dirty man said to his horses. "Whoooa, now."

"Who are you and where do you think you're takin me?" I asked, makin my voice sound stronger than I felt. Talkin made my head hurt even more.

He turned, grinned a tobacca-stained, crag-toothed smile, and said, "Don't act so high and fine with me, girl. I know your kind. Sneakin around, helpin slaves run away from their rightful owners."

Mama, I thought, help me to not be afeared.

"The idea," I said. "I would never help slaves run away from their owners. My father and mother wouldn't never forgive me for that."

The dirty man jumped over the side of the wagon, grabbed his rifle, and walked back to me.

"Well, look-a-here," he said. "You're right fetchy and fancy in all your fine clothes. I couldn't see last night when I follered you from the railroad house." His red-rimmed eyes run all over me, bonnet to boot.

"You and them people in that railroad house are hidin slaves and helpin them north," he said as he walked closer and lifted my bonnet. "I'll get me a good reward for turnin you in." He let go of my bonnet, and it slipped down over my hair.

I were boilin up mad. "I weren't one of them helpin slaves," I said angrily. "I don't even know what a railroad house is. I walked past a few houses, then went to the meetin church for quiet afore my mother and father come to take me to Philadelphia. They goin to find you and send you to jail."

"If you wasn't one of them, why'd you hide?" he asked, walkin around me, and pokin at me with the barrel of his rifle.

"I were sittin in the church when you come in. I got scairt. Folks been sayin that men are comin in from Rogue's Holler and stealin from people. You hurt me, hurt me bad!" I shouted. "My father'll have your hide!"

He shook his head and walked over to a group of men who had turned our way when I yelled.

Purple asters and goldenrod in the meadow to the east of us swayed and bowed in the breeze. A kettle of buzzards glided overhead in wide, lazy circles. As they flew, their long wings tilted and wobbled like they was goin to fall out of the sky. I felt some relieved that they was too far away to pass their unlucky shadows acrost me.

The loop of birds grew smaller and smaller, until one after another landed on the ground and walked acrost the field to a small hump.

"Shag Honeybone," a tall, ragged man shouted, "you done us no danged good here. The poster said to bring him back alive, but you whipped him to death."

Whipped him to death. Who had the dirty man whipped to death?

The fat, chuffle-jawed man beside him, called Micajah by the others, were dressed for a Sunday. He shook a sausage finger and said, "We're not goin to see a penny for that one, but least we didn't have to bury him. Them buzzards are takin care of the carcass." He spit a wad of tobacca onto the ground and nodded toward the meadow.

Carcass. The man had said *carcass*.

I looked back at the meadow. The big buzzards formed a thick black wall. Their heads dipped and bobbed, dipped and bobbed.

"That old Quaker woman ain't goin to make it either. Might as well haul her out to the field too."

That old Quaker woman? Did they mean Auntie Theodate?

The men walked to a wagon, let down the back gate, and dragged out the body of a tiny silver-haired woman.

I heard a voice cry out. I'd know that voice anywhere.

Zenobia run toward the wagon, run till the chains round her ankle jerked her so hard she fell to the ground.

One of the men picked up a shovel that leant against a tree. He walked over to Zenobia and swung.

I screamed afore it come down on her.

The lark is a mediator between heaven and hell.
If you hear the lark sing, you must utter
"I choose heaven" if that is where you wish to go.

The man stopped in midswing.

"Don't you dare to hit my slave girl!" I shouted. "She's near breedin age. Can you pay my father a thousand dollars for her?"

Zenobia pushed up from the ground and turned her head toward me. Her golden eyes looked dead.

The man set down the shovel and swiped his sleeve acrost his sweaty face.

"This girl and a boy was took from my mother and father's farm, stolen from my mother and father's farm. They been missin near a month."

"What's their names?" the shovel-man asked.

"Her given name is Zenobia. Our boy's name is Bright-well. Did you steal him too?"

At the sound of her name, Zenobia turned toward me.

I'm some sure she wouldn't never think that I would be all drest up in such finery and right in the middle of this hornets' nest of trouble. And me claimin to be her owner.

All the men set to talkin. Zenobia were lookin at me, her head cocked to one side. I cupped my hands around my mouth while the men shouted at Shag, and I whistled the lark's song. From somewhere nearby, a lark answered. Out of habit, and for the pure luck of it, I whispered, "I choose heaven."

None of the men noticed the lark's song, but Zenobia nodded her head. She knowed who I were.

Two of the men walked over to Zenobia. Would she remember the name Auntie give me? One man grabbed her by her hair and yanked her head back.

"What is yer name, girl?"

"My name Zenobia. I always has belong to Miss Abigail's family." She pointed to me.

I breathed again.

The men walked back to the noisy group and set to talkin again.

The big man who had knocked me out and hauled me to here turned and asked, "Then why was she and the boy hidin at the Quaker woman's house?"

I walked right up to him, put my hands on my hips the way our neighbor lady Mrs. Stone always done when she were piqued, and looked up. "I cain't say why they was in a Quaker house, but they was took from our farm a month ago. Slave traders come through late one night and stole them from us. My father said he thought they wanted to move them further south so's they could sell them to someone else, but they belongs to us."

The men huddled round me the way them buzzards ringed the carcass in the meadow.

"A fine pot of boilin pig gravy you got us into here, Shag," the fat man said, a brown drizzle of chewin tobacca trackin down the stubble on his creased chin.

"Miss, Miss whatever-your-name—why should I believe anythin you're tellin us?" he asked.

I laid my hands wide open and said, "Because I'm tellin the truth. Now ask yer Mr. Shag Honeybone what he done with my travelin sack. You'll find your answers inside it."

"Shag, go get her sack and bring it here."

Shag walked acrost the clearin to the front of his wagon, reached under the seat, and pulled it out.

I were some happy to see it and to see one patched arm of my Hannah doll pokin out of the top.

Shag dropped the sack onto the ground in front of me. The circle of men closed in.

I reached inside, felt for the envelope, and pulled out the letter.

The fat man took it from my hands. I could see his face changin—it moved from mad to worried, then right on back to mad again.

"Shag, look what you done. Now, how we goin to keep on with that slave girl of hers? How we goin to keep on with her?" He pointed his fat finger at me.

My heart dropped. What if he thought to feed both me and Zenobia to them buzzards?

"That old woman's house is a railroad stop," Shag said. "Nobody saw me pick up the slaves and the old Quaker woman, and no one saw me take the girl from the town. She's mine now, and so's her slaves. I gets the money for them all."

*A green measuring worm is sent
by the devil to measure someone for their coffin.*

"We gots to get movin," the fat man said. "Now load that girl onto your wagon, but put her up front on the seat and tie her feet good. Don't let it show that you got her tied. We're nearin an ordinary where there's bound to be travelers. Further down the road a piece there's a town. This part of the road will have more folks travelin it."

"Where's the rest of my catch?" Shag asked. "I got my list here for keepin track of ones I caught."

Shag pulled a folded paper out of his pocket and read aloud:

" 'Armour Washington. Black. One eye missin, scarred on back.

" 'Enoch Smith, about twenty years old. Light brown. Branded on right cheek with owner's CW initials.

" 'Zenobia, fourteen years old. Dark brown, amber eyes. Scarred on wrists and back.

" 'Better Smith, about seventeen years old. Mulatto, blue eyes. Whip marks on her legs and back, three fingers missing.

" 'Brightwell, tall, black. Scarred on back and face. Long scar under arm to waist.

" 'Theodate Hague. Abolitionist wanted for aiding fugitive slaves. Five feet tall. Sixty years old. White hair. Blue eyes. Private reward.' "

The slaves rose as they heard their names called—exceptin for Brightwell and Auntie.

"Brightwell," Shag called, "Brightwell."

Micajah walked over to Shag, spoke to him, and stood there watchin me.

Shag shook his head and said, "Oh, that were the one," and kept on talkin to the man.

I looked around for Brightwell, but he were nowhere to be seen. Auntie laid on the ground at the foot of a broad walnut tree, her eyes closed, her knees drawed up to her chest.

Shag herded the silent men and girls into the wagon and tied them to the sideboards. Nobody said a word. Zenobia looked over at me, her face wiped clean of feelin. Afore Shag jumped back down, I heard a sound, metal on metal. He had snapped fetters around the left ankle of the branded man, Enoch, and to the right ankle of the one-eyed man called Armour.

"Pick up your bag," Shag said. "Get movin." He thumbed toward the wagon.

I stopped walkin and pointed to Auntie. "Don't leave that old woman out there. That's a waste of a reward."

"She'll be dead in a day. Might as well leave her out with the other," one of the men said, noddin toward the meadow. "We cain't get no reward for catchin her if she don't make it back."

"Put that old woman in the wagon with us, and I'll get her fit," I said, "and you'll get your reward. I just need some food, water, and a few herbs."

The men talked together, then nodded in agreement.

Shag yelled to me to set my travelin bag below the seat. I walked over and slid it underneath. Afore I turned back, I felt inside the hidin place for my knife. When my hands wrapped around the long wooden handle my grandpa had carved, I felt like I were startin to set things to rights. I slid the knife down between the seat and the side of the wagon.

Shag and two other men carried Auntie over and throwed her into the back like a load of firewood. I shuddered when I heard the thud of her hittin the floor.

Auntie never moved—never opened her eyes—never made a sound. I watched Zenobia. A fat horsefly lit on her face. She didn't blink.

All the men walked to their wagons and climbed in.

The horses stirred and lifted their heads as though already feelin the road home under their hooves. One by one the wagons turned and headed south.

"Afore you tie me up, I want to see if that out there is my parents' boy Brightwell." I nodded toward the meadow.

"See fer yerself," Shag said.

Mama, I thought, give me strength. I reached into my pocket and rubbed my thumb against the buckeye.

I walked through the meadow toward them bald-headed buzzards. They saw me comin, fixed me with their dead, dead eyes, hissed, grunted, and barely moved away from whatever they surrounded. It didn't take me but a blink to know that it were Brightwell.

"Oh, Brightwell," I cried. "Oh, oh, Brightwell." He'd helped me, but there weren't nobody by his side when he needed help. Now all the help in the world would come too late for him. My heart felt like it were broke into so many little pieces that nothin could ever make it come back together again. How had all the good slipped so far away?

I pushed the tears off my cheeks and turned back toward the wagon. Somehow I'd get even with Shag Honeybone, somehow and soon. I didn't want to meet Zenobia's eyes. She'd surely see that my hope were lyin back there in the meadow and give over to that death band of buzzards.

Shag spent some time tyin my feet to the buckboard. Then he covered them with my travelin sack. Nobody lookin would ever know that I were a prisoner too. I spread my feet as far apart as they would move and struggled to set them loose, but the knots held. Now I knowed how Zenobia and Brightwell and all them others felt when they was all chained and tied up and treated worst than animals.

Shag circled the wagon and bent to look at a rear wheel. Afore he come alongside to climb in, I looked back at Zenobia. She lifted her head and stared at me.

"Don't worry," I mouthed. "Don't worry."

⁓

Each hoof fall led us further south—and further from free soil. We were at the tip of the devil's tail, the last wagon in the line. The old road were so rutted and dry that the wagons ahead of us disappeared in a rollin cloud of dust so thick that we couldn't see nothin in front of us or on either side.

Shag slowed the horses and drawed back till we was out of the dust and far enough behind so's we could breathe pure air again. He dipped his dirty fingers into a small tin of snuff and stuffed it into his bulging cheek.

The sun beat down; I thought I would die from my achin head and the heat and thirst. I looked back at the others; all but Zenobia set stock-straight, never movin or showin any feelins. The sweat run down Zenobia's neck and her clothes stuck to her. She leant forward, her shadow shelterin Auntie from the sun.

"When are we stoppin for food and water?" I asked Shag, who never bothered to look my way.

"When I say it's time," he answered.

That man were meaner than a snappin turtle with bear teeth.

"If you want me to save that old Quaker woman so's you can get a reward, you're goin to have to find a stoppin place and let me tend to her."

"When I say it's time," he repeated.

"I needs a drink and some food, and I needs to tend to some other things too."

Shag looked over at me, turned his head, and spit an arc of tobacca over the side of the wagon.

"You're nothin but trouble. I should've left you out in the field with the dead slave boy," he said.

Dead slave boy. Dead slave boy. Please, Lord, take Brightwell to your heart. Why did the last thing he knew on this earth have to be more hate and more pain?

"Miss Abigail," Zenobia called. "Miss Abigail, this old woman need some help."

I looked over my shoulder. Auntie shifted beneath Zenobia's shadow.

"Shag Honeybone, this will all be worth your while when you collect the money for the runaway slaves and her," I said, pointin back to Auntie. "You best stop soon."

"Whoa, whoooaaa," he called as he pulled back on the reins and headed the horses toward the shade of trees.

We were so far behind the other wagons now that we couldn't even see their dust.

"You stay put," he said to me. "I got to go tend to myself now."

He pulled back on the reins, the horses stopped, and Shag jumped over the side.

When he disappeared into the woods, I turned in the seat and said, "Zenobia, I gots my knife here."

Zenobia and the others looked up at me. She nodded, then pointed toward the front of the wagon.

Shag walked toward us and said, "There's a house over to the east. Woman workin out in a garden. We're goin there to see what she can spare for us—don't matter if she can spare it," he said, "we'll jus hep ourselfs."

"Well, I cain't go nowhere so long as I'm tied to this seat."

He walked over to my side of the wagon and leant in to untie my feet. A green measurin worm had dropped from the tree and onto him. It humped up, stretched out, humped up again, and walked along between his shoulder blades, measurin him for his coffin.

I reached down, grabbed the handle of Grandpa's knife good and tight, and lifted it above his back.

Leaflets three: let it be.
Berries white: run in fright.

Auntie's words "Thee cannot overcome evil with violence, nor violence with evil" come into my head. I did not want to be no better than my enemy. I lowered my hand, slid the knife back into its hidin place, and watched Shag untie me.

We'd been headin south for a couple of hours. My feet was numb and not wantin to hold me when I stepped down from the wagon. I stomped them to get the blood movin and reached for Shag's jug of water.

It near turned my stomach to think that my lips would touch where his had been just a minute ago. I wiped at the top, gulped a mouthful, and let it run down my dried-out throat. I took another gulp, swallowed, walked to the back of the wagon, and climbed up onto it.

Shag had his back turned to me. He were bent over and lookin close at the horse's hoof.

I pressed the jug to Zenobia's mouth and let her drink her fill. Then I moved over to Auntie and poured a thin stream of water onto her face and neck. She moved and opened her blue eyes, blue eyes that looked as empty and lifeless as Moses's cat eyes.

I lifted her head, held the jug steady, and offered her a drink. She shook her head no.

"Yes, Auntie," I whispered. "You needs to drink a bit and get your strength."

Her eyes focused on me. She opened her mouth and drank. I felt hope trickle into me as sure as the water that run down her throat.

"Get it up and move it," Shag yelled at me as he walked to the back of the wagon. "I don't want no dirty slave mouths touchin my jug. They's a bucket back there for them under the wood lid."

I slid the lid off. The water looked green, murky, and it stank of a pond. I reached for a small tin cup, dipped it in and held it, one by one, for Armour, Enoch, and Better. They sipped greedily and tipped their heads to me in thanks.

"The woman ain't in the garden now. You go on over

to that cabin and ask for food and water. And I don't want you lettin on about anythin in case they's sympathizers," he said.

I slid out the back of the wagon with the jug in one hand and patted Auntie and Zenobia with the other.

"I'll walk alongside the wagon," I said to Shag as I neared his seat.

"Might as well," he said. "Don't want to spend no more time tyin you when we're just goin down the road a bit. Remember though, you run and I kills that slave girl you's spendin so much time on."

"Why would I run?"

"You'd run so's you could go free and stir up more slave trouble."

"Mr. Honeybone, my father and his men will be findin us soon. You'll be in sore need to do some explainin."

Shag spit, clucked his tongue at the horses, and shook the reins.

"I'm not worryin none about them findin us. We'll be south too deep for them to track us."

"They won't stop till they find me," I said in my most growed-up voice.

The pair of bay horses moved forward fast. "Whoaaa!" he said. "Settle down now." The horses slowed and the one on the left looked back at Shag, the whites of his eyes showin all round. He looked scairt and I saw why. A cart whip set in its holder within reach of Shag's huge hand.

"Keep up to me," Shag said, "or, fetchy and fancy or not, you'll get a feel of the whip."

For once, I kept my mouth clamped shut.

The wagon rolled down the road toward a farmhouse surrounded on two sides by woods. A kitchen garden stretched from a lopsided barn to a stone springhouse. I stepped lively to keep up with Shag, which weren't so easy to do in fancy shoes. I wanted to take them off but knowed that a barefoot lady wouldn't set right.

Shag pulled to the side of the road and headed toward the house. He stopped short of it in the shade of a tree. I walked to the bed of the wagon and looked over the tailgate. Zenobia leant against the sideboard with her eyes closed. Auntie's silvery head rested on Zenobia's lap.

Looked to me like Auntie had a bit of life pinkin up her cheeks. She turned her head toward me and smiled. I saw the spark back in her blue eyes, and it made me feel right better. Maybe Auntie just needed a tonic, food, and rest to set her back to rights.

"Now you git over to that house and ask them what victuals they has. Tell them we're headin south to home. They don't help us I'll take what I need, and I don't give a wad of spit about them people. Remember, you say any-thin about me bein a slave hunter and the girl'll be feedin buzzards—and so will you."

My hands curled into tight fists that wanted to punch at his face.

"Mama, please, please help me find a way through all this," I whispered.

I set my bonnet to rights and tied the ribbons. I didn't think anyone way down here would be lookin for a runaway redhead, but I remembered Auntie's cautions.

When I reached the farmhouse, I knocked loud and called out a greetin.

The door swung open and a young woman not much older than Zenobia answered. She had a round-faced baby settin on her hip, and her arm were hooked through the high handle of an oak-splint basket.

"Oh," she said, her hazel eyes wide in surprise. "Company! I don't get many folks stoppin by here. We see folks passin by on the road, but hardly never stoppin."

"Good day," I said. "We're headin south and I'm in need of fresh water and a few victuals. And I got a sick auntie in the back of the wagon. I'd like to make up a tonic for her if you has some healin herbs to spare."

All the time I'm talkin I'm prayin she has somethin for us and thinkin to myself that there weren't no way I'd let Shag hurt this woman and her little boy.

"Y'all feel free to go out to my garden and pick yourself anythin you need. I got a lot comin on—ripe tomatoes, corn, snap beans, herbs—go see for yourself."

I breathed some easier, and I could feel the peace settlin back onto me. My fists uncurled.

She slid the big harvest basket off her arm and passed it to me. On the way to the garden, she stopped at a line full of work clothes and gathered them into a bundle. Son on one hip, washin on the other.

A flock of chickens scratched in the dirt, and a rooster stood atop the stone springhouse watchin over his hens.

I looked toward the wagon. Shag were tippin up what looked like a flask. Zenobia were still, her eyes closed like she wanted to keep all the world from gettin into her. The girl Better looked over at me, but the others stared straight ahead.

"I'm sorry not to be rememberin my manners," the girl said as she piled her clean clothes into a big willow basket. "I'm Emma, and this here is Little Will, named after his pa." She follered along behind me as I picked, sharin the daily trials of bein a mother and the loneliness of livin so far from a town and her family. Most of the news she had come to her from German merchants and settlers travelin on the wagon road between Pennsylvania and the Carolinas.

I loved the music of Emma's voice and the sound of Little Will's liltin *coo, coo, coo.* He sounded more like a mournin dove than a baby.

After a few minutes of gatherin, I follered the girl to her little patch of healin herbs and picked a few handfuls of the plants my grandpa had taught me to use. First Melissa and valerian root for sleepin and calmin. Then sage, peppermint, spearmint, and some red-flowerin bee balm, enough so's I could brew up a good tonic to give Auntie some strength.

At the side of the herb garden, a fat tangle of poison ivy wound its way up a tree. I walked over to it, the smell of the herbs under my feet risin up, and stood thinkin on the ivy's wicked power—a power strong enough to change life for me, Auntie, Zenobia, and the others.

Below the tree, a tall stand of orange-flowered jewelweed hummed with bumblebees. I yanked off a handful of the leaves and bent to the job of pickin off the knobbledy red fingers that circled the stem a few inches aboveground.

Emma looked on, frog-eyed, as I rubbed the jewelweed leaves and red fingers acrost my hands, neck, and face.

"What you doin?" she asked.

"Gettin ready to pick me some poison ivy. It don't never bother me, but I'm takin care jus in case it acts up on me this time."

"You cain't pick that poison ivy," she said. "Why, you'll be all boiled up faster than a kettle of water."

"Don't worry for me," I answered, "but I'd much appreciate a little piece of sackin for the pickin and to carry some of them leaves."

The girl shook her head side to side like I were right crazy, walked into her barn, and come out with a holey grain sack. I tore off a piece of the cloth and used it to pull some of the leaves from the vine. Ten, eleven, twelve sets of shiny triplet leaves lookin so safe, safe as the herbs I'd gathered for Auntie's tonic. I closed the cloth over them, folded it into a small square, and tucked it up into my sleeve.

I looked around the corner of the cabin. Shag were tippin again, and when he finished, he tossed the flask over the side of the wagon and laid back in the seat.

Emma led me acrost her garden and toward the springhouse. We stepped over a scramble of goose grass, the same as what my grandpa used for cheese curdlin, and its tiny, stickery burr seeds stuck to my skirt. She pulled at the door latch of the springhouse, and it swung open slow. Cold air and the smell of butter and cheese met us. Little Will, still settin on her hip, leant out toward me, and I scooped him into my arms and passed her my empty water jug.

When I started to step inside, she ducked her head like she couldn't look straight at me, and said, "Y'all wait out here." She come back outside carryin my jug filled to the top, a cold milk tin beaded with water, and a big hunk of somethin wrapped in a bright-blue bandanna. "Take these too. Maybe someday y'all come on back and say hey to us." Emma's hands shook as she tucked each of her offerins into the big basket. What had got into her to flighten her up like she were?

I couldn't make her a promise I might not ever be able to keep. "I'll never forget your kindness. I hope to do somethin for you someday," I said, a wash of tears fillin my eyes.

The three of us started headin toward the wagon. "You'd best stay back," I cautioned. "He is right mean all the time, but bad mean when he drinks."

Emma stopped. Will reached for his mama, and she lifted him out of my arms. I felt sad to let the sweet softness of him go. He raised a small pink hand as if he was wavin a good-bye to me.

When I got close to the wagon, I saw Shag's head was throwed back and his eyes closed. His Adam's apple moved up and down, up and down, as he snored. I crept past him. He snorted, and his eyes opened and rolled into his head till they disappeared. My heart were flutterin inside me.

I unloaded the herbs, food, milk, and water into the back of the wagon while Emma and Little Will watched me from the big stone step in front of the springhouse. I lifted a hand high and gave a wave afore settin their empty basket at the foot of a nearby tulip poplar tree.

Auntie still slept, but Zenobia and the others watched silently as I walked to the side of the wagon and reached for the bedroll below Shag's outstretched legs. He moved, groaned, shifted his feet, and brushed one foot against my hand. I stopped and waited to see if he would wake. He snorted again. I sniffed at the sourness of his sweat mixed with whiskey—the smell of my pa.

I picked up the bedroll, backed away from him, and laid it on the ground. After I unfastened the leather cinch and unrolled the blanket, I pulled the square of cloth from my sleeve.

Shag's head lolled to the side, facin right at me. He stirred and scratched at his stubbly chin.

"Leaflets three, set us free," I whispered as I unfolded the cloth and shook the poison ivy leaves into the beddin. I laid one blanket against the other and kneaded it like I were makin bread, then shook the oily leaves out of the bedroll afore cinchin it closed.

At the side of the wagon, I stooped and looked, figurin the space I needed to get the bedroll back in its place. Shag moved his feet and drew them beneath the seat. I stopped and waited. He moved again, then straightened his legs. I bent over, judged at the space, and jammed the roll beneath the bench. I almost made it.

When smallpox strikes someone,
you must drive the demon of it
into a sow and burn the sow to ashes.

Shag opened his runny, red eyes, yanked the whip from its holder, and shouted, "Girl, what you think you're doin?"

"Jus makin a spot for the victuals," I said quiet-like, though my heart beat so hard I were sure he could hear every thump.

"You're not givin them no food," he growled. "We leavin here. Get back on the seat."

He set up, slid the whip into its holder, and fumbled for the reins.

"They needs to eat if you're wantin to get any reward."

"They can eat, but not till after I gets mine. You feeds

the animals last. Now shut yerself up and git me some food."

I walked to the back of the wagon, tugged off the heel of the bread, opened the blue bandanna, and pulled out some cheese and a tomater. Right beside the bread I found some thick slices of ham. Emma's heart were big—bigger than mine. I left the ham for the others.

Zenobia and them were watchin me, watchin that pile of food I fixed for Shag.

I whispered, "We'll eat later," and looked up to see if he were lookin. Then I spat onto his tomater and cheese and watched my venom spill onto the bread.

I were hungerin too. My stomach felt like it were eatin itself, bite by bite, till there weren't nothin left but empty achin.

I laughed and quick covered my mouth. Just leave it to me to laugh at the wrong time.

"Don't talk!" Shag shouted. "You talk at her again and I'll whip you and them." I couldn't hardly tell him that I weren't talkin, but laughin at what I done.

I shuddered thinkin of that nasty whip in the wagon.

"Git up here. We puttin some road under us afore you eat," he said.

I looked back at Zenobia, but her eyes was closed again.

The horses moved along steady, the wagon swayin and creakin. Shag held the reins in one hand and stuffed food into his mouth with the other. He reminded me of our mean old sow, Daisy.

We traveled for a few hours till the sun rested atop the western mountains. I'd be right happy to see it set after such a long, hot ride. I couldn't wait another mile and begged him to stop so's I could tend to some necessaries and get food together for us.

He grunted, reached along the side of his seat, and pulled out another flask. "I wanted to catch up with the others afore nightfall, but it looks like they's too far ahead. We'll make camp here tonight," he growled.

Shag headed the bays off the dusty road and over to a small clearin bordered by a stream. He unhitched the horses, picketed and hobbled them, then yelled to me to fix him somethin to eat. The horses set to drinkin and browsin; Shag just set to drinkin.

I were pickin through foodstuff, tryin to decide how to make supper for everyone, when Shag picked up his whip and rifle and walked to the back of the wagon. He untied one end of the rope holdin the line of slaves together and yanked it hard. One by one, Enoch, Armour, Zenobia, and Better slid from the wagon and onto the ground, but Auntie laid there, eyes closed, and still curled up like a fern frond.

"Git over to that tree," Shag ordered, follerin behind with more rope.

The line of them walked slow, Enoch and Armour clankin in their fetters, nearly fallin. The girl Better was draggin her feet behind Zenobia, who walked sure with her head high.

Whoosh, crack, the whip sounded its warnin.

One by one they sank to the ground and watched as Shag tied their ankles and hands tight together. How could they stand the bindin and the pain?

پ

Shag set under an oak, his back against the broad tree. He gnawed at some bread and drank from his flask—his eyes never left us.

"Y'all stop watchin me," he shouted.

I walked over to him, lifted the jug settin beside him, and poured water into a tin cup. "I'm right glad we aren't with everyone else. I heard from that girl back there that some of them German folks from a town up north got the pox."

Shag's eyes widened and one of them twitched fierce. He started to say somethin and opened his mouth afore swallowin what he'd just drunk. The whiskey poured over his lips like a millrace. His shirt were soaked through.

"The pox? We got the pox here? This ain't worth all the trouble I go through. No reward's worth the pox." He took another swig from the flask.

"My grandpa called whiskey the water of life," I said in a treacly voice. "He used it to clean wounds and to cure most everythin."

Shag gulped another mouthful. This time all the corn

whiskey went down his throat. I were glad for that and hopin that it would send him to sleep.

I moved over to the wagon and gently nudged Auntie. "Auntie," I said, "Auntie, wake up now. You needs to drink and eat. You needs your strength."

Truth be told, I needed Auntie to get back her strength. I missed her.

I propped up Auntie's head and let her drink her fill, then I fed her tiny bites of bread and ham.

When I finished feedin Auntie, I picked up the bucket of water and lugged it over to the others, who were whisperin amongst themselfs. When I knelt down to dip a cupful of water for Zenobia, she asked, "What about Brightwell?"

I just looked at her and said, "He's gone." She shook her head slow and tears filled her eyes.

The words had just come out of my mouth, and Shag were up and walkin over toward me sidewise, like the old yeller dog that got bit by a sick skunk last summer.

I set the bucket down and moved away from Zenobia afore Shag come closer.

He made it another few steps, stumbled, and grabbed the wagon's side.

"You, girl, you. I told you no talkin."

The sun dropped below a notch in the mountains, and Shag looked around, like he were surprised by the dusk.

"I'm goin to sleep," he said. "We're leavin early tomorrow. Git over here, girl. I'm tyin you to the wagon."

"But what about all of us eatin? We starved and thirstin."

I started to say more, but he raised his fist the way Pa does to let me know what's comin.

"Where am I spost to sleep?" I asked, knowin that none of us would see a spoonful of food.

"I'm tyin you up on there," he said, pointin up to the wagon seat. "And don't you be talkin to them."

I climbed onto the seat and he bound my feet together, then tied my hands behind my back.

He stumbled to the other side of the wagon and pulled his bedroll, rifle, another flask, and a small cookin pot from under the seat. Shag made his camp over by the side of the crick near a lopsided circle of stones filled with the charred wood of an old fire.

He mounded kindlin and branches inside the stones and fanned at a small flame. We watched as he took a big swig from the flask, then another, and another—corn squeezins spillin down his front with each gulp.

"Keep your eyes to your own business," he yelled, "or I'll pick them eyes right out of your ugly black heads!"

Shag kept drinkin, and the little cookin pot never were put into use. After a while he lifted his shirt over his head and draped it onto the branches of a sweet pepperbush all spiked with flowers.

I watched as he undid the cinch around his blankets and rolled them out onto a grassy patch of ground. When he climbed inside the bedroll, he took a big swig from the bottle and laid back, cradlin his rifle in the crook of his arm. Within a few minutes, he were snorin loud, the bottle capped and lyin acrost his hairy chest.

I looked up at the darkenin sky filled with birds headin to their roosts. They swooped down together, hunnerts of them, like they was one bird, and flew into the trees around us. Then they all joined together talkin and tellin of the day's happenins, then everythin were quiet like they had disappeared.

Zenobia, Armour, Better, and Enoch, all of them tied together under the tree, hummed quiet amongst themselves like evenin bees. Then everythin were quiet. Quiet like they had disappeared.

Behind me in the wagon, Auntie slept, but I didn't think I could never sleep bein all tied up. But I must've, cause I were dreamin about me and Zenobia trapped in the cave when I woke to a screamin that could rouse a rock.

"The pox!" Shag yelled. "Lord a'mighty, I got the pox! Someone needs to burn me a sow to ashes."

*The dragonfly is a "snake doctor" and will hover above
a snake, protect it from harm, and sew it up after injury.
It may even bring it back to life.*

My neck, so stiff I couldn't hardly raise my head, felt sore from the long night. I turned and looked over at Shag. He surely did look like he had the pox on him.

Eyes swolled to little slits; face puffed up and red with weepin spots; hands, chest, neck, and back all broke out in a rash—if I hadn't knowed better, I'd a thought the pox too.

Durin the night, my hands come free. I reached down and untied the ropes around my feet. Shag were too sense-less to see that I were loose without him even havin to untie me.

I looked back at Auntie. She were sittin up! Sittin up

and lookin most like her old self. And Zenobia, over there with the others, she wore a big grin acrost her face like none I'd ever seen.

My feet near didn't hold me when I climbed down from the wagon and turned toward Shag. He were runnin at me—flappin and squawkin like the worn-out hens I axed for dinner.

"Whoa," I said as he got closer. "Whoa, I'll tend to you with some herbs, but you cain't get close by them or me. We cain't take care of you if we get the pox. Now go lie down and I'll try to help you."

He finally paid me some attention and set right back down on them poison ivy blankets, yellin, "Don't just try to help me. I'm on fire, on fire! Do somethin. I'm dyin."

"You are in some sad shape, Mr. Honeybone, but I'll fetch some herbs and tend you. You're doin nothin but makin it worst bad for yerself."

Next when I looked, Shag were rollin around on the ground like an upside-down cooter turtle. He whined and cried and scratched at hisself all over. He took a long drink from his flask, then another, and another afore he laid back on his bedroll and closed his eyes.

I couldn't feel no pity for him.

I walked to the back of the wagon with the water jug and give a drink to Auntie. She drank deep, then leant back against the side rails and watched as I gathered up food and water for the others and carried it over by the tree where they was all tied.

My grandpa's knife sliced easy through the ropes around Zenobia's hands. Soon as she were free she worked at untyin all the others.

"Some water in the jug and milk in the tin," I told them. "And ham under the bread, and there's cheese, green beans, and tomaters." Zenobia and Better opened the blue bandanna, tore off pieces of bread, and set slices of Emma's ham on each one. I couldn't stop myself from stuffin my share into my mouth.

Zenobia shook crumbs out of the bandanna, folded it into a triangle, and tied it onto her head. When she tucked her wiry brown hair under the bandanna, she didn't look like the Zenobia I knowed.

We all ate in quiet, couldn't say a word or hear a word with Shag startin up again with his moanin and cryin.

"I'm dyin. Dyin, with the pox!" he yelled.

I looked over at Zenobia and smiled.

"Sweet girl," Auntie called. I were some surprised to hear her voice strong for the first time in days. She were up, had slipped out of the back of the wagon, and were walkin slow over to us. She smoothed at her skirt and pushed wisps of her flyaway silver hair out of her face. I loved it when she called me by the very name my grandpa once used.

"Lark," she said, "thee is causin that man great pain. Thee should treat thine enemy as thee would thy friend."

I am not kind as Auntie. I were likin the sound of Shag's misery and felt like he were bein punished for all the bad he done to the slaves he caught, whipped, and killt. He couldn't be hurt near enough for what he done to my friend Brightwell.

I picked up a piece of bread, laid a slice of ham on it, and passed it over to Auntie.

She reached out, took it into her hands almost like she were prayin, and smelt of it afore takin her first bite. Then she lowered the bread, looked at me with her cornflower-blue eyes, and said, "Sweet girl, thee must minister to the man or I can't eat this food in good conscience."

She wanted me to "minister to the man"? The same man what hunted slaves, chased, beat, and sold them like they was animals, and killt them like they was nothin. I'd as soon try to put gloves on a rooster.

I took time eatin my last bite of bread and brushed crumbs off my skirt as I walked toward Shag.

The fire beside him still showed some life. I added dry kindlin to the embers and fanned it with my fancy bonnet. It didn't take but a couple of minutes for the fire to come on, and then I laid it with some twisted branches till it flamed high.

"You ain't worth spit snuff!" he yelled at me.

I didn't need to hear them words from him; I'd heard

them plenty from my pa. But then, he were the same kind of man as my pa, with the same stream of mean, strong-as-snake poison runnin through his blood. Were there some bad runnin through me that roused them to be hateful? Or were it the whiskey turnin them cruel?

I picked up Shag's pot and walked to the wagon for some of the herbs Emma had shared. But I'd need me some pain-killin willow bark from the silvery-green thicket by Shag's camp.

The willows was lively with the worried rattlin and chatters of tiny, black-masked yeller birds who picked through the branches for bugs. I whistled soft to soothe them, and their worry calls turned to their *witchity, witchity* song.

I rolled up my sleeves and used Grandpa's knife to peel long strips of willow bark. *Plink, plink, plink,* I dropped them slivers into the pot till it were halfway filled.

Right above me a white-tailed dragonfly, each of its clear wings patched with two black spots, hovered and dipped. Grandpa called them snake doctors. He told me they tended after snakes and would hover above them in the fields. I looked close at the ground around me. I learnt to always watch where I were steppin when I saw one of them snake doctors close by.

When I got back to Mr. Shag Honeybone, he were in a fitful sleep. A blessin for him and for us too. He turned, tossed, tried to get up and walk away, but I pushed him down and told him to stay put. I added some valerian root to the pot of willow bark, set it on the fire, and watched back and forth between Shag and the pot as the water simmered and turned the color of a muddy crick.

"Mama, Grandpa, what should we do now?" I asked.

I couldn't think on where we could turn or how we could all get away from the hunters out on the trail. How long afore someone in the long train of traders turned back to look for Shag?

The pot of herbs bubbled, and the driftin smell reminded me of my grandpa. I bent to stir down the boil and saw Shag's rifle lyin next by him like a wife. I carefully slid it out from the crook of his arm, carried it over to the wagon, and tucked it under the seat beneath a ragged blanket.

I were worried, but now I weren't worryin alone. Now I had Auntie again, and Zenobia and the others, but now I had all the others to worry for and to hide. What if we got caught and sent south?

"I'm jus a twelve-year-old girl." I must've mumbled that aloud to myself, cause Zenobia's gold eyes got big and she looked at me like I were crazy.

The words *Armour Washington, one eye missin; Enoch Smith, branded; Zenobia, scarred on wrists and back; Better, three fingers missing; Theodate Hague, private reward* was burnt into my mind like the CW letters on Enoch Smith's cheek.

"Moses," I said. "Mama, I got to remember Miz Moses. She done it and so will I. Step by step, mile by mile."

The sounds come to me, but I weren't payin attention to nothin ceptin my own thoughts. Then Zenobia grabbed my arm and held her hand behind her ear.

"Horses," she said. "Horses comin on, and comin on fast from the south."

*To stomp your right foot three times
is good luck, but to stomp your left foot is bad luck.
Turn around three times to unwind the bad luck.*

The others quick set down against the tree, and Zenobia worked at fixin the ropes so's they looked all tied together. At the end of the rope, she looped it round her legs and stuck her hands behind her back. I'd cut the rope too short for her to tie, but she grabbed it and held on.

Auntie run for the wagon, bent over and picked up somethin from the ground, then crawled into the back. She stretched out straight, eyes closed, and placed a flat death rock on each eye.

I rushed to my sack and pulled out another one of my new long dark skirts, shook it open, and laid it over Auntie's body.

Hooves pounded along the road, and I heard someone shoutin, "Here they are, here they are."

Two men rode in and stopped next to the wagon. I knowed the tall gray-haired man with the beard. He'd been a part of the group of men movin slaves south. His broadaxe face would be hard for me to forget. But the short, fancy-dressed man in the wide-brimmed white hat hadn't been with the slave catchers or traders I'd seen. He spun his sorrel mare and looked over the camp-site.

"What you doin way back here? Where's Shag?" the fancy man asked. "You supposed to be behind us, headin south."

"I wouldn't get no closer," I said, starin up at them straight in their eyes. "We got the pox here and more. We travelin this road with a mess of death. Now the old woman is dead of the lung fever, and over there is Mr. Honeybone—near dyin too." I pointed to the lump of blankets acrost the clearin.

The men seemed like they was weighin out my words one by one, like coins.

Above us a sparrow hawk screeched like a lost haint. "More bad luck," I said.

The man on the sorrel looked up, then rode over to the wagon and used the butt end of a whip to lift the skirt off Auntie's face. He quickly pulled the whip back, and the skirt dropped down over her.

"I don't believe it about Shag," the broadaxe man said.

"I'll warrant you killt him." He turned his horse around and walked it over toward the mound of beddin where Shag were sleepin.

He got down off the horse and lifted the edge of the top blanket with his foot.

"Whoot!" He let out a yell that would stop a chargin bear. He stepped back, both hands over his mouth, and stood there like a seed takin root.

I could see them blankets movin, then Shag set up and said, "Help me, help me, I'm dyin. I got the pox." He tried to push hisself up, but fell back down. He were some sight.

The fancy man on the sorrel whirled round and took off at a gallop. His hat flew off and wheeled acrost the clearin. The other man backed up till he near bumped into me. When he got to his horse, he almost didn't make it into the saddle. Last I saw he were headin south.

Shag kept yellin till he found his flask and took three long gulps. Then he settled back into the very blankets poisonin him and closed his eyes.

After the riders left, I stomped down on my right foot three times. "Good luck, good luck! We had us some good luck! Finally."

Zenobia let go the rope and helped the others work their hands free. They all walked over to me—Enoch and Armour clankin together with every step. Auntie set up straight, the skirt slippin off her face and them death rocks clatterin onto the floorboards. Enoch reached over the end of the wagon and helped Auntie out.

We stood there lookin at each other, knowin that somehow we'd managed to trick them men that was searchin for us. Shag Honeybone, who'd gotten us all into this predicament, were who saved us.

〜

I sank down onto the ground beside the wagon and Zenobia set next to me. Auntie leant against the backboard and watched us. Armour, Enoch, and Better talked quiet amongst themselves.

"That were too close for me," I said to Zenobia and Auntie.

"My heart's still poundin," Zenobia said, "but we made it, and we's safe. Now what we goin to do?"

"I knows what we goin to do," Enoch said as he and Armour walked over to the wagon and rummaged through the pack Shag had stored under his seat.

"Here it be," Armour said. He held up an iron key and bent to unlock the fetters.

Snap. The two men stepped free.

Armour walked acrost the clearin, picked up the fancy man's white hat, and whacked it against his leg till he raised a cloud of dust. He set that hat on his head, looked over to us, and smiled. He looked right fine.

"*Now* what we goin to do?" Enoch asked.

. What we goin to do? When Zenobia and Enoch said them words, I felt as weighed down with rocks as the bag my pa used to drown our spring kittens.

"Let's think on this," I said. "We done fine with Shag havin the smallpox. Instead of actin like we runnin, we should act like we have sick folk with us. People are scairt unto death by the pox."

"Thee is right, Lark. Nobody expects runaways to travel by day. We'll go north in the day instead of travel-ing by night."

"Hidden in plain sight—ain't that right, Auntie?"

She nodded. "Hidden in plain sight is our best hope."

I looked down. Me and Zenobia set next to each other, our arms wrapped around our legs. Her arms was the color of dark clover honey, mine pale, white, and freckled like a wood thrush's chest. I had forgot that we was differ-ent colors.

I heard a sound behind us. Someone stumbled, swore. I looked back over my shoulder.

Whoosh. Crack!

Shag Honeybone, lookin worst than death and barely able to stand, come runnin at us with his whip.

*When a sperrit tickles your spine,
no good will come of it. Say "Go away, sperrit,"
and ask a friend to brush it off your back.*

I remember the sound of the crackin whip and how Zenobia grabbed my arm and tried to pull me along with her and the others, but I couldn't move. Everythin went quiet and slow. Then I saw Auntie run toward me, and Zenobia pulled at me and screamed for us to run.

When I looked down at my skirt, there were a long, wide tear acrost it. I felt blood oozin from my legs. It spilt warm and slow-like and made its way down my skinny shanks, soakin into my stockins and my fancy shoes.

Whoosh. Crack! The sound come again, but this time I felt the whip bite into my arm and coil round it like a black rat snake.

I pushed myself up and stumbled. The whip stayed wrapped around my arm. I run toward Shag Honeybone, who were near to fallin down, grabbed the handle of the cart whip from him, and shoved him hard. When the whip loosed on my arm, I raised it to strike him. I wanted him to feel the bite of the snake.

"Lark," Auntie said, "thee must hand me the whip."

"I am no Quaker, Auntie. This time he should taste of his own punishment."

Auntie faced me and put her small hands on my shoulders. "I'll tend thy wounds, but thee must cast away the whip. I think that thee already doled him punishment enough."

Shag squirmed on the ground, writhin like a worm cut by half. Next I knew his eyes closed and drool run from the corner of his blistered red mouth. He were right sick.

Auntie took the whip from my hands. Armour, Enoch, and Better come from the woods toward us.

Zenobia and Auntie was tuggin at Shag's legs, tryin to pull him to his camp but gettin nowhere. Armour reached down, picked up Shag's whip, and threw it near to a tree. Then he and Enoch each grabbed an arm and a leg, and hauled Shag back to his blankets.

Zenobia put her arm around my waist and helped me walk. We stopped by Shag's bedroll and looked down at him. All I felt were a hate and mad that made me want to hurt him worst than he'd ever hurt anyone. The mad and hate burnt in me—burnt and turned dark. I could taste it, a taste like the bitter water that come up from my stomach when I were sick.

"Mama, Grandpa, will I go straight to hell if I hurt Shag? And if I went to hell, then Grandpa, how would I ever see you again? How would I ever get to meet you, Mama?"

I looked down onto a body pocked red and oozin from every sore. His corn whiskey flask set on its side, half empty. I picked it up, opened his puffy red hand, and tucked the whiskey bottle inside.

Then the pain come bad and I blacked out.

꒰꒱

Zenobia and Auntie took off my shoes, walked me into the slow-movin crick, and washed at the deep, burnin red stripes acrost my legs and arm. One lash and both legs was cut near to the shinbone. I must've held my arm in front of me when I heard the sound of the whip. The bloody red welt curled up and round and round.

Zenobia stood with me, her legs crissed and crossed— marked by scars tellin the same story of cruel. My legs and arm hurt beyond the ken, but still, they weren't nothin when I put them side by side with the scars that Zenobia and the others wore.

I tried to walk but hobbled like a three-legged hound.

I don't like feelin useless, but I couldn't help myself. Armour lifted me into his arms and carried me to the back of the wagon. I stretched out, laid my head on my travel sack, and held on to my Hannah doll's arm.

Auntie disappeared into the woods and returned with some freshly gathered witch hazel. She emptied Shag's pot of willow bark and valerian root into a tin cup and brung it to me.

"Here, sweet girl, drink this, and I'll make thee a poultice."

Havin Auntie in my life must be like havin a mama.

She drew some crick water for the pot, tossed in the witch hazel, and set it to boil on a flame started with embers from Shag's campfire. Zenobia climbed up and set next by me, coaxin me to drink the tea. Auntie dipped two pieces of cloth into the pot of witch hazel, used a twig to lift them steamin-hot rags out, cooled them for a minute, then laid the poultices on my legs and arm. They stung fierce bad, but I clamped my teeth closed and never made a complaint.

When Auntie finished tendin me, she brewed a tea strong enough to set Shag to sleepin for a day and a weaker draught to help me sleep through some of my pain. Enoch and Armour picked up Shag, blankets and all, and moved him deeper into the broody woods, where nobody passin by on the road would see him. Enoch set to tyin Shag to one of the trees, wrappin him like a moth caught in a spiderweb, but Auntie stopped him.

"Thee mustn't hurt him or tie him, or thee is no better than the slave catchers. We'll leave him be and head north toward home. We'll travel in the light of day," Auntie said.

⟫

Enoch climbed up and onto the seat beside Armour. Better, Zenobia, and Auntie climbed into the wagon bed and set around me, layin out a portion of Emma's food for our supper.

Armour, in his fancy new white hat, took the reins and *cluck-cluck*ed the horses into movin. They slowly circled the campsite, then headed north on the rough, dusty road.

The healin tea, the witch hazel poultice, and the sounds of my friends' voices set me off to sleep. I woke surprised that it were dark and wonderin why my legs and arm was hurtin me so bad. Then I heard voices and saw Zenobia and Auntie and the others settin round a fire. I laid on my back lookin up at a coal sky sprinkled with stars. I counted seven for good luck afore I turned onto my side and listened to their tellin of the happenins of the past weeks.

"I gots our freedom papers sewed into my pant leg," Enoch said.

". . . don't matter none that we're free. That slave hunter say I run from North Carolina to New York with my wife. Fugitives . . ."

I could hear someone cryin.

"Slave catchers come into our house middle of the night, put us in chains . . ."

"In chains," Better said. "Our family don't know what happen to us."

". . . holdin on to our papers. We'll go back home. Free. Again . . ."

Free. Again. Free.

I laid there listenin to Enoch's voice risin up and down like a hymn. His words settin pictures in my mind. When I closed my eyes, I saw silver minnows swimmin against the rushin water, leapin, dartin into the shadows, slippin into the sunshine, silver minnows all of a body, flashin in the light, searchin for the safe.

Better settled down next to Enoch and said, "Oncet we shows them the papers, they jus take them . . . and we cain't prove we free."

Armour said, "I don't have no papers. I run from Mississippi."

"I lives in swamps, hides in pigpens and haylofts, sleeps in muddy ditches, bit by every crawlin thing, travelin at night . . . always at night."

"Made it all the way to Pennsylvania when that man Shag dug me out of a haystack and whipped me some good. You know the rest."

You know the rest.

Life with Pa and my brothers were bad. No love for the findin. But all the time the bad happened I hoped that someday I could be free. Zenobia, Brightwell, and Armour, they never felt that hope. They was slaves. Bought, sold, and owned like they was no better than a hogshead of molasses. They didn't have no hope for nothin more. I didn't know if I could go on livin without the hope for more.

Auntie walked over and patted at me. I struggled up and rubbed my eyes, then slid off the tail of the wagon to the ground. Everythin spun around me, but I hugged onto Auntie and made my way over to the fire.

Our wagon—Shag's wagon—were pulled up under trees, out of sight of the road. I didn't know how long I'd slept, but the day were done and I were starvin.

Zenobia moved over, and I set down with her. Auntie brought me corn bread, ham, and some wild berries she must've picked while I slept. I chewed slow, still listenin, puttin pieces in place.

We talked on till the last log were tossed onto the fire. When everyone seemed played to the end of the spool, Auntie said, "Now thee will sleep safe. Tomorrow morn we'll start north before sunrise and travel in plain sight."

What if Shag wakes up and finds help? What if Pa and my brothers sees us? What if the slave hunters come back? I knowed what would happen to me if we was caught, but in the worst, darkest parts of my mind, I couldn't even think of what would happen to the others. I felt a shudder run up my spine like a sperrit were ticklin it.

"Zenobia," I said as I leant forward. "Will you brush off my back? I feel somethin crawlin." She brushed at me till I felt the sperrits leave.

We said our good-nights, each of us carryin a heavy load of worries and fears. Enoch and Better held hands and walked over to a clutch of trees. Armour leant against an oak with Shag's whip in one hand and his rifle standin up against the trunk next by him. The last of the fire flickered acrost his face, and the fancy white hat perched on his head. I felt some safe havin him there, watchin over us.

My legs, burnin and achin like they did when Pa whipped me with his rawhide, barely held me up. Zenobia and Auntie helped me to walk and to climb back into the wagon bed. It made me mad to feel so helpless. We curled beside each other and pulled the ragged blanket over us. Skeeters sang their whinin songs in my ears, and around us, the thick hot night rasped and trilled with the sounds of the dog days' bugs.

I don't know what woke me—a noise? A dream? I set up, my legs and arm throbbin. It took me a minute to remember where I were and what happened to make me hurt so bad. I looked around the campsite and could still see the dyin orange coals of the fire and the white of Armour's hat against the darkness of the oak tree. I settled back down on the hard wagon bed and laid betwixt Auntie and Zenobia.

Low in the gray mornin sky, the hunter Orion rose with the bright star Sirius follerin below. A horse nickered. I set up again and looked over at the oak tree. I rubbed at my blurry eyes, squeezed them together, and looked again. Where were Armour? Had someone caught him and carried him away? Or worse?

The wind combed through the leaves. A twig snapped. *Clank.* The sound of metal hittin stone. *Click.* The sound of a rifle hammer cockin.

*Whatever you do to a robin will be
done back to you—break an egg and something of yours
will be broken. Always tell the robin "good day" when you see it
or hear its song, and your luck will be good for the day.*

Scufflin sounds, then Armour's voice, deep and clear.
"Stop."

Then two, maybe three voices wound all together.

Zenobia woke; Auntie mumbled and turned over.

"What?" Zenobia whispered.

"Somebody here, in camp. I heard Armour yell. Heard people talkin. We best hide."

I moved the blanket aside, and Zenobia and me both set up. She leant over me, squeezed Auntie's shoulder, and whispered, "Wake up, Auntie. Someone here."

One by one we slid off the back of the wagon and crouched low. Anyone acrost the clearin wouldn't see us.

We hunched over and made our way toward cover. I were slowin them down, but they wouldn't let me stop—Auntie holdin on to my good arm and me holdin on to Zenobia. We needed to get out of the clearin and into the woods.

Who had tracked us or found us here? Now what would happen?

Orion disappeared. Long wisps of clouds, the mottled gray of Moses cat, lightened, their bellies turnin pink and rosy.

We stepped from the dirt of the clearin where the wagon rested and into the soft, leaf-strewn gloom of the woods. Ahead of us, a cluster of boulders stood beside a deer trail. Auntie, Zenobia, and me climbed the back of the biggest rock, stepped over the top, and worked our way down to the cool, mossy shelter on the other side.

More sounds. Cracklin of someone walkin, steppin on twigs. The crunch of leaves and snappin, then what sounded like a pebble skitterin. More sounds, like there were more than one man stalkin—maybe two or three.

Long as there were only one I felt like we had some chance of hidin or runnin, but three changed things for us. Three men the likes of Shag and his kind, and the three of us—me barely able to walk, Auntie just gettin better, and Zenobia with her broke arm tryin to help the both of us.

From somewhere behind us, I heard more footsteps. Hushed talkin in deep voices.

The three of us held hands and hunkered back against the big rock.

Zenobia's eyes was squeezed shut. Auntie faced to me, shakin her head a slow no, no, no.

I wanted us to get up and hightail it, but when I tried to, Zenobia pulled at me, tuggin me back to the ground.

How long afore the slave hunters found us? Tracked our six footprints acrost the clearin, into the woods, and here.

I thought of all the times me and Zenobia hid together. In the cellar, in the cave, in the trees, and in the attic of Auntie's house. Here we was, hidin again. Always hidin, always afeared, always runnin from someone. When could we ever stop runnin?

No more voices. No more sounds of walkin. Was someone out there just waitin for us to move? Waitin like a barn cat after a mouse? Did Armour tell them he were alone? Where was Enoch and Better now? Already caught? Or scairt and hidin like us?

One of the old bay horses neighed. I heard the sound of quiet talkin and the clink of metal. I smelt a quickenin fire and heard the wake-up call of the robin.

I thought, Good day, robin. Help us change our luck.

More clinkin metal. Were someone hitchin up the horses? Takin Armour and Enoch, Better and the wagon away?

After a few quiet minutes, Zenobia opened her eyes and whispered, "I think we safe."

I started to breathe again. Started to think on how we

would keep walkin north, maybe not in plain sight like we'd planned, but headin north somehow.

More noise. The horses movin slow. Voices. Voices louder, closer.

Then a scramblin sound of someone crawlin up the side of the big rock shelterin us. The little hairs on the back of my neck bristled like they do when Pa is watchin me.

Zenobia reached for my hand and squeezed. I reached for Auntie's hand and held on.

Then a *scratch, scratch, scratch* on my head and shoulder, and a leafy twig of an oak tree, its little acorns just startin to plump, dropped beside us.

*Avoid gray horses with four white stockings.
They are bad omens.*

I tilted back my head, and there, starin at me all upside down and grinnin, were a face I never thought to see again. I gasped. "Sweet living Lazarus." I dropped Auntie's and Zenobia's hands and jumped up, coverin over my mouth so's not to yell.

"Why you hidin from me?" he asked.

Zenobia, Auntie, and me leant into Brightwell's big outstretched arms, all huggin and cryin at once.

When I stepped back and looked at Brightwell, my stomach turned and twisted. His scarred face had even more sores, and his arms showed fresh whip marks crusted with blood.

"What happen to you?" he asked me, lookin at my arm.

"Looks like the same happen to me as you," I said, "but worst on you than me. I thought you was dead. I thought they hauled you out in the field and let them buzzards eat you down to the bone."

Brightwell helped me, Auntie, and Zenobia over the boulder, then we all walked back toward our camp. I couldn't help but notice how he limped and favored his left leg, and how he held on to his arm.

"Shag whipped me good and left me lyin by his wagon. Them men took one look at me, say I a dead man, and hauled me out to the field."

"But I saw them buzzards come for you. I watched them buzzards round you."

"You saw them lookin for a meal, but I weren't their meal that day. I just had to stay there till them slave traders leaves. I hear you call my name, hear you cryin, but I didn't dare to move or call out."

I remembered how them buzzards circled, looped, then dropped down into the meadow. Their big bodies made a black wall of death around the hump–the hump that were Brightwell.

"I kept liftin my head, tellin them wrinkled old buzzards that I weren't ready for them yet. Every time I talk at them they look at me with their big, starin brown eyes."

I looked up. Above us, nine death-bird buzzards, their long black wings spread wide, circlin in the blue August sky. I made a wish and watched for one to flap its wings to make it come true.

Flap, flap, flap. Three flaps. Three chances for our luck to change.

"Them buzzards sounds like devils moanin, gruntin, and hissin at me. Sounds like I never hear. They smell rotted. They peck at me with their big hooked beaks."

Auntie patted at Brightwell's shoulder. "It is good to see thee again. I hadn't even a hope of seeing thy face again after the beating that man gave thee."

"I were right lucky, Auntie. Conductor found me where I'd crawled into the woods. He give me water and food, and tell me the signs to foller to a stop on the railroad. Good folk there hid me, took care of me."

Zenobia had listened quietly. "I'm glad you think you lucky, Brightwell, but I'd say you was not lucky to be beat near to death by that man. Hard to remember them 'good folk' when so many bad are after us," she said.

"But there are the good people who don't believe that a person can own another, Zenobia," Auntie said.

Zenobia slowly shook her head back and forth. "Ummm, ummm, I hoped that freedom time were comin, Auntie, but that slave law and them bad people took away my hopes."

"Hope all we got, Zenobia," Brightwell said.

"Brightwell, how'd you know you might could trust them people?" I asked.

"Hope. When I get there, I watch, pray, and hope I'm not steppin into a trap."

I reached for Zenobia's hand and squeezed it tight.

"The night I were leavin the safe house, a wagon with three other runaways come in for help. A young woman, Miss Emma, brung them from her farm down the road."

Emma. Emma were one of them good folks.

"Lark, Miss Emma say you stop for food and water and then head south with a wagonload of people. Then she say next day or so she saw your wagon goin by headin north, but she didn't see you nowhere. Worried you was hurt, or, or . . ."

Zenobia and Auntie looped their arms through mine to help me walk.

"When I leave the safe house, I went north after your wagon. I wants to find you all, wants to catch up to him and reckon an eye for an eye. By the time I finds him, finds where he were sleepin, he were so sick, all pocked up and out of his head, I just left him be. Left him to suffer like he left me."

"You won't be catchin what he had," I said. "I give him a dose of poison ivy. Poison ivy and corn liquor is what made him out of his head."

Brightwell laughed and said, "I follered the wagon tracks all night till I found your sleepin spot. I knowed Shag were left behind, but I needed to make sure you was alone."

"Thee has found us now, Brightwell, and we will all travel north together. Peacefully," Auntie said.

Peacefully? I were right sure that Brightwell weren't feelin much peace for Shag and for the likes of him.

We reached the campsite and found Armour, Better, and Enoch all cleaned up and waitin by the wagon, the horses hitched and ready to go. Better handed us each a wedge of corn bread topped with the last of the ham. One bite and it were gone—my stomach wouldn't be stoppin its complainin.

Brightwell knelt by the crick and splashed his face and arms. Then he picked through Shag's pack and pulled out an old tan shirt. When he lifted it over his head and tugged it down, well, he looked like any free workin man.

Armour slid the rifle behind the wagon seat. Brightwell and Enoch climbed up beside him while Auntie, Zenobia, Better, and me crawled into the back and set our minds to the day.

Enoch lifted the reins, clucked soft to the horses, and turned them round.

"We needs to be movin on now," Brightwell said. "Better and Enoch are a free man and woman goin north to Auntie's farm. They gots their manumission papers and can show them off to anyone who asks. Me, Armour, and Zenobia, we don't have no papers, so we say we belongs to you, Auntie."

He said all that to us like he were preachin a sermon. It calmed me some to hear how sure his voice sounded.

The wheels jolted as we moved onto the rutted road and headed north. The sun rose higher in the sky, and the day, like most dog days of August, were hot enough to bake corn bread on a rock.

We passed the tin of water round when the heat got us near droppin, and Auntie pulled bits and pieces of food together, then handed them to us. We was near out of food, and I could hear Zenobia's stomach growlin, but food were the last thing we could be worryin about now; we was gettin closer to a town, and we was bound to see some other folks soon.

The sun blazed, and the smell of pines, a smell I always loved, near made me sick.

"Someone up ahead," Brightwell said as he looked back over his shoulder at us. We leant out over the side of the wagon and saw the dust risin along the road. Who would we be meetin? Did we look like runaways or could we pass ourselfs off as just folks headin north?

"Hidden in plain sight," Auntie said to us. "Remember, thy journey is home to Waterford."

Brightwell nodded. Nobody made a sound.

My foot set to twitchin, wigglin back and forth like it always done when I get to frettin.

Meetin a wagon weren't scarin me. That were what I kept tellin myself. I tied the ribbons of the fancy bonnet tight under my chin, tucked in my red hair, and set up straight. Auntie, Zenobia, and Better brushed themselfs off and leant back against the rails, their faces set.

My heart took to flutterin. I looked round, but not one of the others seemed a mite scairt. I sure weren't goin to let on how I felt.

"Mama," I said, "I could use me some good luck. Couldn't you and Grandpa help us?"

The wagon rolled closer and closer. Soon I could see one man drivin and one man sittin beside him with a rifle acrost his lap. Close behind follered a man on a big gray horse with four white stockins. Bad luck come ridin right at us.

Fridays are a bad-luck day to laugh.
If you laugh on Friday you'll be crying by Sunday.

The wagon and rider passed by. Armour stared straight ahead. Me and Auntie raised our hands in greetin. As the man on the unlucky white-stockin'd horse trotted past without another glance, I felt like a thick barrel band had loosed and dropped off me. When I looked back over my shoulder, I saw the rider rein in the horse and swing it around.

"Stop!" he yelled. "Where you headin?"

Enoch called out a soft "whoa" and pulled back on the reins.

The man on the white-stockin'd horse rode back by the

wagon, circled the front, looked the men up and down, and leveled his rifle at them.

Auntie stood up and greeted them. "Good morning, Friend," Auntie said, like she were talkin to her favorite neighbor. "Won't thee please move aside and let us pass? We are hurrying home to tend sick family."

I knew that just tellin that little lie, even though she were tellin it to save us, would trouble Auntie.

"We're not movin anywhere but where we want to be. And where we want to be is right here, askin you who you are and where you're goin," the man shouted. He moved his rifle till it stared at Brightwell.

Sweat soaked through Enoch's shirt. He looked back at us, his eyes wide, but when he saw the fear on Better's face, he turned and said, "Sir, please, she tryin to get home to family. We be travelin hard since North Carolina."

"You don't talk at me, boy!" the man shouted.

The rider come closer and looked over into the bed of the wagon where we set.

"Lift them blankets," he ordered.

I couldn't get up, but Auntie bent over, picked up the mound of blankets, and laid them over the side of the wagon.

The rider poked at them, rode around us, and set his rifle back acrost his saddle.

"We've had runaways on the road and up on the Blue

Ridge," he said, "but we catch most of them at night, when they thinkin they safe. Stupid, stupid slaves. That's why they slaves, they stupid!"

Brightwell leant forward. I knowed him and knowed that after all he'd been through he'd like nothin better than to yank that man off his horse. He started to stand.

Auntie walked a step to the back of the wagon seat and laid her hand on Brightwell's shoulder. "Thee has a spacious heart—let it fill with the Light," she said quiet-like. He settled back.

I were shakin, some sure that if Brightwell had done what he wanted to do, well, there would be plenty of blood spilt to pay for all of our pain.

"Go on," the rider said, lookin us over again. Then he nodded north, the way we was headin.

I couldn't help myself and let out a small snort of a laugh. Auntie shook her head at me, and Zenobia's golden eyes widened in surprise. I bit at my lips, covered my mouth, and acted like I'd just sneezed.

The man stared at me, turned, dug his heels into the horse's side, and rode south. But he left his white-stockin'd bad luck behind when he tipped his hat and said, "Good Friday to you."

Oh law. I'd laughed on a bad-luck Friday. I'd be sure to be cryin on Sunday.

"Get ready," Enoch said. "Down the road a ways they's

some more people and two riders. We run into them soon."

Better squeezed her eyes shut. Auntie set between Zenobia and me and held our hands. Were there any way we could come out safe through this? All we could do was roll on, right into the middle of trouble again.

Avoid riders on white horses or you will surely run into bad luck or death.

I couldn't stay jus settin. Settin and waitin. I stood up behind Brightwell and looked at the road ahead of us.

"Oh no," I said. "Brightwell, here's Armour's hat." I snatched the hat off Armour's head and passed it to him.

"It's the woman-man, the very same woman-man what caught you."

Brightwell pulled the hat on and slunk low on the wagon bench. He kept his head down so's she couldn't see his scarred-up face.

I stepped back and set down in the wagon again.

"Zenobia, remember that meaner-than-a-mule-bite woman-man? Under the sycamore tree? We in for trouble."

Zenobia nodded. "What happen to our luck?" she asked. "Best make sure you still has your buckeye." She sank down, pulled the blue bandanna low on her head, and swiped her hand acrost her shiny face.

Better didn't move, didn't neaten up, didn't show any feelins. It were like Better were with us, but her soul had left her.

Auntie set up straighter, smoothin her plain skirt, and tuckin and twistin her hair into a small coil.

I needed to make myself feel peaceful so I checked again and made sure every wisp of my red hair were still under my bonnet. Then I patted at my pocket to feel for my buckeye and set up prim and straight like the young wife of our travelin preacher. "Please, Mama and Grandpa, help us make it through this safe."

The riders and three boys moved slow, but we all come together at the place where a small trail run into the wide road.

The woman-man on her white horse and the weasel-face man on the chestnut geldin stopped, yelled somethin at their boys, and watched us passin by.

I cast my eyes down. I didn't want to look at the boy with the chicory-blue eyes. Please don't let them remember Brightwell. Don't let them boys remember me.

We rolled slowly past. I felt all them eyes starin at us, starin into us, like they knowed that we was shirkin from them.

"Where you headin?" the woman-man asked.

The wagon stopped. Auntie stood.

"Hello, Friends," she said. "We are traveling from North Carolina to our home. We have some sick family."

Poor Auntie. I knowed it pained her.

The woman-man shifted on her saddle and craned her neck till she could see into the bed of the wagon. She circled us, stoppin at the tail end, then stoppin by the side of Enoch and the others.

"You, you in the hat. Lift it up. Lift up yer hat."

Brightwell set still.

"He can't hear a word thee said. He is stone deaf and dumb,"Auntie said.

"You, boy"—she pointed to the dirty boy with the chicory-blue eyes—"lift his hat and let me have a look at him."

The boy stepped up to the side of the wagon and started to climb onto the seat.

Enoch shook the reins and clucked for the horses to move.

"Stop!" the woman-man said. "Go after em!" she shouted at the weasel-face man on the horse.

He turned and rode toward us.

The boy had held on to the side of the movin wagon. He swung up, reached for Brightwell's hat, and tugged.

"It's him! It's the slave what run away from us!" he yelled over his shoulder.

Brightwell reached out, grabbed the hat, and pushed the boy off the wagon and to the ground.

Seemed like the world blowed to pieces round us.

Shoutin. Better screamin. Enoch shakin at the reins, horses boltin forward, and the man aimin a rifle right at Armour.

Then I heard them. The dogs. Grandpa's dogs— Bathsheba and Delia. They was soundin their chirpin barks and bayin and makin enough noise to raise the dead.

I looked down the trail to the side of us and saw Pa, Samuel, and Clem runnin fast toward us. Trouble. More trouble.

Zenobia started to crawl over the side of the rail.

"No," I said, "you cain't get away now. Them dogs would find you. Pa would shoot us. It's too late, too late."

I pulled her back into the wagon.

"We gots to set still and keep quiet."

Zenobia settled next by me. Auntie stood and looked toward the three men headin right at us.

"Curse you two!" my pa shouted.

Had he already seen me?

"You, woman. What you think you doin? You tryin to catch my runaway and git the reward?"

He were talkin to the woman-man and weasel-face.

I watched from under the brim of my bonnet. Pa and my brothers didn't know I were in the wagon. Them dogs hadn't smelt me yet.

"That boy up there is my catch," the woman-man said.

"I had him till he broke free and run away. Now I got him back."

"I don't know about no boy. I'm trackin a runaway slave girl. She's my take."

"If she's a runaway with a reward, then she's mine," the woman-man shouted.

"Thee must let us pass," Auntie said. "We are traveling back to our home and sick family."

"Git out of my way!" Pa yelled to the woman-man as he started toward us.

I didn't dare look up, didn't dare let him notice me.

The dogs was barkin and runnin around the horses.

Pa yelled at the woman-man again.

"Woman, move away from that wagon!" Pa shouted, motionin with his old shotgun. "I'm lookin for the slave girl with the big reward."

"One more step and you're dead. I'm sick of you and yer kind stealin from me," the woman-man said as she pointed her rifle at Pa.

Just then Delia and Bathsheba lifted their muzzles, sniffed, and went crazy wild. They circled the wagon, barkin, leapin up at the tail end, tryin to get to me.

"I knowed it!" Pa yelled. "They found the slave girl. She's mine. We gittin the reward."

He moved toward us and Brightwell stood, towerin above Pa and all the others.

"That's him, that one's ours!" the woman-man shouted, aimin at Brightwell.

I stood up and reached behind the wagon seat where Armour had hid Shag's rifle. None of my friends could use that rifle against any whites, no matter how bad them people was. My friends wouldn't never get their freedom or find shelter with anyone if they was killers. They'd be hung from a tree branch like a shot deer.

My fingers wrapped around the barrel. I lifted the rifle up and over the back of the seat and held it out of sight.

"Git down here, boy!" the woman-man shouted. "Right now, reward or not, I'm shootin you, you miserable . . . Do somethin!" she screamed at the man who rode with her. "Do somethin, you stupid, worthless fool."

The weasel-face rider looked at her, turned his horse, spit a brown stream of tobacca, and rode away. He yelled back over his shoulder, "I am sick of bein your stupid, worthless fool. Find someone else."

While the woman-man watched us, the three white boys, the ones who had been under the sycamore tree, took off runnin in three different directions. The chicory-eyed boy ran north, the white-haired boy run south, and the other, he just run, zigzaggin like a rabbit runnin from a fox.

She screamed at them, "Worthless cowards. All! Worthless!"

The rider and the boys never stopped. Never looked back.